Fake it to the Limit

MARY FRAME

 Created with Vellum

This book is dedicated to my children, Cole and Lorelai, for whom I would do anything.
Except clean your bathroom because you guys are gross.

Chapter One

MAKING a deal with a teenage girl is like swimming with sharks. Minus the cage.

"I know it stinks, Paige, but you have to stay hidden. You have to promise. Pinky swear." I hold up my hand over the cracked center console between us, pinky curved in the universal symbol for sisters everywhere.

I glance over at her in time to see the eye roll, a gesture that's been occurring with more and more frequency with each mile that we've put between us and our parents.

"I'm not going to ruin this, Charlotte. I'm not an idiot." But she links her pinky with mine for a brief shake before returning to what's been her permanent pose for the last eight hours: staring out the dusty window with her knees drawn up to her chest.

"I know you're not. But I also know you can't sit still for more than five minutes and this might take a while."

"I don't get what the big deal is. I'm not a little kid."

She's not. She turned thirteen six months ago. There's no more baby fat, just gangly limbs contrasting with her slightly curving figure. My little sister isn't so little anymore, much to my chagrin. It was so much easier only a few short years ago when her biggest concern was how much candy she could sneak from her Halloween stash. Now she's wearing bras and stealing my makeup.

"I know." I avert my eyes from the road long enough to see her dismayed expression. "But we can't risk losing this opportunity."

The ad was very clear, as was Ruby when I talked to her on the phone briefly. No children. No pets. Free rent in exchange for maintaining and preparing the property for when the owner returned from her hiatus.

We couldn't pass up this deal. A solid place to stay, a roof over our head for four months. Even if the place turned out to be a dive, anything would be better than the seedy motel we had been occupying for the last two weeks. After we bought the car, a withered old sedan without a radio or air conditioning, we didn't have much left. Almost nothing.

Paige blows out a breath that sends the long, dark lock of hair always hanging in her face momentarily airborne.

"Fine," she says. "But you owe me."

I don't respond. We're both silent when we turn the corner and head down the main street of the town we'll call home for the next four months. To our right is the boardwalk, littered with bright dots of people and charming shops. Beyond that is the ocean.

Castle Cove is like one of those towns you see in magazines about the best places to live, with shiny pictures of happy people and quaint streets.

This is where our lives will truly begin. A place where we'll be safe. Normal.

"We're almost there."

"Ugh," Paige says, but she climbs into the back seat and lies on the floor, covering herself with a blanket without me having to ask.

Only a couple of blocks past the boardwalk, I park in front of a small brick house. It's a narrow two-story with a sagging porch and a yellowed lawn, but it's real and it's ours. Definitely not something our parents would have chosen to live in. There's nothing that screams wealth and luxury. If it spoke at all, it would be a faint hum of meek and tiny.

I take a deep breath.

This is our new life. It's going to be great.

Ruby Simpson isn't what I expected. I imagined the owner of a new age shop would be older, with fuzzy hair and a horde of cats. But Ruby is young and petite, with blond hair like mine, except hers is a natural golden that flows around her shoulders like waves of honey. Mine came from a bottle and probably looks like it hasn't been washed in three days.

Because it hasn't.

She's probably only a year or two older than my own age of twenty-one.

I wish I could be travelling, touring the world without a care. People my age are going to frat parties and making bad decisions. I'm raising a teenager.

"I'm so glad you could be here on such short notice, Charlotte," she says. "I wish I could stay and open the shop. Tourist season is coming, but I couldn't turn down the Dalai Lama."

She's wearing flowy clothes and a mess of colorful bracelets that jangle on her wrists when she waves them around, completely distracting me from her words.

I nod and avoid direct eye contact.

Ruby is a spiritualist. She's opening this new age shop, Ruby's Readings and Cosmic Shop—the sign should be coming soon, she tells me—but she can't stay. She's been invited to an ashram in India to meditate with the Dalai Lama. Hence the need for a renter, and quick.

So quick she arrived in town yesterday and she's leaving . . . hopefully soon. I feel terrible that Paige has to stay in the car under a blanket. Thankfully it's cool enough this time of year that I don't have to worry about her dying of heatstroke.

Ruby had me sign the lease agreement and employment forms, then made copies of my ID and social security card—fake, naturally. Now we have less than an hour for her to show me around and tell me what I need to do while she's gone.

"This is where the shop will be," she says, indicating the dusty front room with a sweep of her arm that sends her bracelets jingling. "There's inventory being shipped within the next week, but this space will need to be cleaned before everything is set up. Through here," she walks toward a side room and I follow, "is where I'll be doing the readings. I want to put up a row of beads in this doorway. . ." And so she continues, showing me the house and what she wants done—what Paige and I will be doing—until she returns.

Under the dust and cobwebs, the house is cute, and it's furnished. The downstairs is where the main business will be, which really takes up no more than two rooms—the front room for the shop and behind it a reading room, a small space where she'll need no more than a table and a few chairs. Beyond that, there's a homey kitchen, a living room with a fireplace and wide, built-in bookshelves, and a garden in the yard out back. There's some furniture in the downstairs living space, a worn but fluffy-looking sofa and an old TV.

Upstairs she's showing me the office when a thump sounds from the bedroom next door.

"What was that?" she asks.

"I didn't hear anything."

Dammit, Paige. I should have been more specific. Instead of stay hidden, I should have said stay hidden in the car. She used to sneak around all the time, eavesdropping on our parents' planning sessions. They would often keep us in the dark about the cons they were running, even if they had us working the job with them.

There are no more strange noises as Ruby shows me the software she uses for the business on a computer set up in the office. She also goes over how to scan in invoices and receipts. She's hooked the computer up to satellite—it's already been paid for. She had to splurge a bit for the better connection but the only other option in this area was dial-up.

The set-up is nice. I can tell with just a glance. All top of the line computer equipment, a surprise considering the rest of the surroundings.

Then we head to the master bedroom.

"I'm so glad you found me. It's amazingly hard to find renters on short notice without kids or pets. It's not that I don't like kids or animals," she hurries to explain. "But I need a clear space when I return, and unnecessary auras will affect the feng shui."

There's a muffled giggle from the closet and I cough loudly, trying to mask the noise.

"I totally understand," I say loudly. "Kids are unpredictable and, man, so annoying."

An offended gasp escapes the confines of the closet and I stomp on the floor to cover it. "The floor is real sturdy," I say, practically yelling.

Thankfully, Ruby must not be as psychic as she claims because she doesn't seem to notice.

I ease us toward the doorway. "You said you had a list of things downstairs?"

I'm going to throttle Paige once Ruby leaves.

Downstairs, Ruby goes over the list of items she's expecting, where everything needs to go, phone numbers to call if certain shipments don't come in, plus a list of things to do.

There's an emergency number where I can leave a message, but since there are no phones at the ashram, the number belongs to a store more than a mile away. If I have to call her, it's likely she won't be able to get back to me for a week or more. Just in case, she also gives me a business card for her family's accountant. It's a simple but thick cream card with a fancy font. Definitely old money, I think, fingering the card.

When I go to plug the various numbers into my cell phone, I notice that there's no service.

"Right." Ruby nods and frowns apologetically when I ask. "There's no cell tower nearby. But there's a landline phone in the kitchen and another one upstairs in the office. Feel free to use that if you need to call anyone," she tells me.

I can't really complain. Living off the grid is a good choice. The better to hide away. One of the big draws to Castle Cove—other than the free rent—is the fact that it's practically the middle of nowhere.

Once we've finished all the basics, I help her carry her bags out front, where a long black town car waits to take her to the airport an hour and a half away. She has four giant bags. One for each month?

When Paige and I left for the rest of our lives, all we brought was one small bag apiece.

"Charlotte," she says, squeezing my hand and smiling at me like we're best friends, "thank you. I feel like you were meant to be here. You have such a wonderful energy."

I'm not sure how she knows that, considering I've barely spoken since we met and there's probably nothing positive about my energy at all, but whatever.

She scans my face and then the house behind me. "Don't worry about anything," she tells me. "It will all be wonderful." She hugs me then, her jangly bracelets digging into my side.

I pat her on the shoulder awkwardly.

"See you in four months!" she says, all bright exuberance. Then she's gone, sliding into the back seat of the town car and disappearing into the night.

Chapter Two

"We're registering you for school, not signing you up for a drag queen contest," I tell Paige before she can make it all the way down the stairs.

She's dressed normally enough: jeans, a T-shirt that's a bit too tight, and old, worn Converses on her feet, but her face is rouged and lined like she's going to be selling her wares on the corner.

"You're so annoying," she says, stomping back up the stairs.

I may be annoying, but at least she listened and I won't be walking into the school with a mini-harlot.

I'm standing at what will eventually be the checkout counter, perusing the supply magazine Ruby left. Crystals, herbs, books about enhancing your psychic abilities. What a joke. I flip to the next page.

A few minutes later, Paige returns. She still has makeup on but she looks more like Malibu Barbie than Hooker Barbie, so I'm happy.

The happiness doesn't last out of the driveway.

Whee-whee-whee-whee-whee. Turning the key in the ignition for the twelfth time yields the same result. The car won't start.

Paige and I exchange a glance and then I pop the button for the hood.

She gets out to assess the damage.

"We need oil," she calls from behind the hood of the car. "But my bet is on the battery. The cables are corroded."

"Of course," I grumble. I hop out of the driver's side and glance around. There's no garage attached to the property that might be hiding tools or other potential car-saving items. There's just a tire path to park the car on the side of the house. But our neighbor has a garage. Surely they have a bottle of oil to spare.

I jog up the steps to the neighboring house and rap on the door. From the outside, the house appears almost exactly like ours. Or Ruby's, I should say.

The curtain in a window beside the door flickers, but after a minute of standing around, no answer. I knock again.

Still nothing.

I frown. "No one's answering," I call out to Paige. She slams the hood shut.

"Now what?"

I grab my purse out of the front seat. "We walk."

The sky is gray and foggy as Paige and I head down the sidewalk.

"The view isn't that great," Paige says, her arms crossed in front of her chest, a frown on her face.

"It's early. The sun should burn off the fog eventually."

A runner in gray sweats and a black, long-sleeved shirt runs around us. From the back, he looks young, with a high and tight haircut, broad shoulders, a slim waist, and strong muscles flexing with every stride.

"The view looks good to me," I mutter.

"Gross," Paige says, but she laughs and nudges me with her elbow.

We walk in silence for a few minutes, turning away from the boardwalk and further inland to where the middle and high schools are located.

The streets of Castle Cove are tidy. I can't help but wonder who lives behind each well-maintained yard and picturesque brick home. It doesn't seem like there are many residents out and about this morning, but it's still early. One elderly woman is watering flowers, and an old man sits on a porch, rocking next to a floppy-eared dog. None of them look like they're worth anything. The houses are too old, the flowers too cheap.

I focus my gaze on the sidewalk in front of me. None of that matters.

"I don't have to go to school, you know."

"Yes, you do. We've talked about this, Paige."

It was one of the biggest, most compelling reasons to leave in the first place. I want to give Paige a stable place to live. A normal life. The ability to stay in the same school for more than a few months at a time. Maybe even friends. All things I never had and she's never had the opportunity to experience.

"I know," she says. "But we also need money. I should get a job."

"You're too young."

"I could do, you know, other kinds of jobs."

I halt her progress with a hand on her arm. "We are not doing *other* jobs. We left for a reason. We're not going to be like them. I'll head down to the boardwalk later and find a job.

There's a ton of stores. I'm sure someone is hiring. Our rent is covered. We just need enough for food and essentials. We can save up for a place of our own. It's going to be fine. No, it's going to be great." I smile broadly even though I'm not really sure it's going to be great. But it has to be better than what we left behind. It has to.

"We'll need to fix the car, too," she grumbles.

I choose to ignore her.

The school is closed for spring break. The sign on the door indicates they'll be open again this coming Monday for classes.

"We walked all the way over here for nothing." Paige scuffs her shoe against a crack in the sidewalk.

"Not nothing. Now we know when you start."

"Yay," she deadpans.

"Who peed in your Cheerios?" Seriously. Does every teenager on the planet emit the negative force of a black hole?

"It's nothing." She starts walking.

"Paige. We're supposed to be happy," I call to her back.

"I am happy," she says in the unhappiest tone she can muster.

I jog a little bit to catch up with her. "This is supposed to be exciting. A new start. No more worrying about . . ." I don't have to finish that sentence. "What gives?"

"It's just— I can't— I don't know." Her voice is frustrated.

We continue to walk in silence. I know better than to push. She'll let it out eventually. We talked about escaping from our parents for years, making ourselves practically giddy with anticipation. But ever since we left, Paige has seemed anything but.

We stop at the general store for a quart of oil and it isn't until we're home and working on the car that she finally spills.

"What if no one likes me?" she asks while we're trying to

fashion a funnel out of tinfoil. There was no other way to get the oil in without spilling it everywhere, and the neighbor is still pretending to not be home.

"What?" I ask, having nearly forgotten our earlier conversation.

"What if I go to this school and all the kids hate me? Or think I'm lame? I don't know how to be cool. I don't know how to be anything."

I stand up straight from where I've been hunched over the engine. Paige is sitting on the stoop, her head in her hand and her dark hair gleaming in the spring sunshine.

My hair is the same color, normally. My parents made me dye it. They said blond girls were more attractive. I was never quite attractive enough. Paige and I look a lot alike, but I think she's prettier. Her eyes are a dark blue, as opposed to my brown ones, but we do have the same pert nose and full lips.

"No one is going to hate you, Paige. You're awesome. I would know, we're related."

"You don't understand. You've never had to hang around a bunch of hormonal teenagers and actually . . . be yourself. It's almost easier when you have a role to play or you know you won't be there long. You can pretend like it doesn't matter."

I put the bottle of oil down on the ground and sit down next to her on the bottom step of the porch.

"You're right. My entire adolescence was spent in a new place every month with a new name and personality. And it was terrible. This will be better." I wrap my arm around her thin shoulders. "We have to believe that."

She nods.

"Now why don't you work on the car," I hand her the lumpy foil, "and I'll go down to the boardwalk to see if anyone's hiring. Maybe I can get a job at that candy factory we saw on the way in and you can have licorice for dinner three nights a week."

She rolls her eyes but then smiles slightly and stands. "Deal."

~

It takes less than five minutes to walk to the boardwalk. It's still pretty early, barely nine thirty, so there aren't many people wandering about. Just a few tourists and hungover college-aged kids.

The first three stores I stop at aren't hiring. Neither are the next three, or the five after that.

My final shot is at the restaurant. I ignore the sinking sensation in my stomach. I can get a job somewhere else in town, I suppose, but it would be nice to find a place within walking distance since the car is a question mark.

After getting the bad news from the hostess up front—not hiring—I head around to the back of the restaurant and stare out over the water, letting the salty sea breeze blow away my troubles.

The boardwalk sits near the top of the actual cove. Curving to my left, after the boardwalk ends, are a few houses and some larger buildings in between little snippets of beach. Beyond the buildings, there are more ribbons of beach sand, and in the distance, just before the land arcs to a stop and the sea begins, there's a grassy knoll and the remnants of a stone building. That must be the castle that Castle Cove was named for.

I didn't have a chance to do much research on the town before we moved here. Once I saw free rent and a population slightly under three thousand, I knew we had found a place to go. It was like the universe had pointed us in this direction, if I believed in that sort of thing.

The town itself is located in southern Oregon, on the coast. It's as far away as I could get us from our parents without living under the sea. Paige loves the water, but it freaks me out. I can't swim to save my life.

I'm gazing at the seagulls, wondering how easy it would be to hunt them for food and if I could convince Paige that it's actually chicken, when I hear people talking.

"George, this product is expired," a voice complains.

"It's not expired," George replies. "The boys just caught them yesterday."

I can't see them, nor can they see me, but at the empty section of the walk, their voices bounce around and hit me with perfect clarity.

"Don't bullshit me. I can smell it from here. I can't use this."

There's silence and then, "It's spring break. I have reservations booked through the entire week. How am I supposed to feed people with expired fish?"

I grimace. Gross.

"Well, I can make another run and bring it back but—"

"Forget it. That would take three days and I can't afford to lose business. Someone stole an entire box from my last delivery. And I'm not paying full price either. Bring it into the . . ." Their voices fade as they enter the building.

Note to self: don't eat at the pier this week.

Not that I could afford it anyway.

I continue walking down the pier, leaving the restaurant and voices behind.

Toward the end of the boardwalk, before the shops peter out and the water extends to the horizon, there's a boarded-up storefront. The outline of the faded inscription on the building says it used to be the World's Greatest Sock Emporium.

What a shame it's closed.

I peer into a gray-stained window, but it's too dirty to see inside. Walking around the building, I find a door without a handle and push it open. I can immediately see why it got shut down. Even with just the illumination from outside coming through the dirt-caked windows, it's easy to see this space is unusable. It smells like mold and decay and the wood floor is rotting in spots.

Behind some kind of old, crumbling shelving unit, the front half of a child's red shoe sits alone and conspicuously bright amid the clutter in the dark and dirty building, making the surroundings a bit surreal.

A child's laugh echoes through one of the walls, and I'm immediately creeped the eff out.

That can't be real. It must be coming from outside, but a quick glance behind me reveals an empty boardwalk.

"Is anyone there?" I call.

There's no answer. I move further into the building, then stop and listen.

Nothing, except the sound of my own breathing, the quiet beat of the waves outside, and the occasional squawk of a seagull.

The wood shifts beneath me, groaning as if someone is walking along the corroded boards, but I'm the only one here and I'm not moving.

"You're not supposed to be in here." A loud voice startles

me into a short and awkward shriek. I jump back, my stomach dropping somewhere in the vicinity of my toes.

There's a man in the doorway. Not just any man. It's the runner that passed us this morning, still in his gray sweats and black shirt. Cute butt man. He's even better looking from the front, I realize through the pounding of my heart.

I take in his features quickly, incongruous as they are. His nose is perhaps a bit too large for his face, and his lips are rather thin, but he has a strong, square jaw and intelligence in his too-close-together eyes that make it hard to pull my gaze away. When you put it all together, he is surprisingly attractive.

Then I realize I'm staring at him and he's staring at me and probably expects me to respond somehow.

"There's a red shoe," I say through a dry mouth.

"What?"

"Um." I can't look at him.

His expression is clearly wondering if I have a screw loose and I think that maybe I do. I switch my focus to the wall and bite my lip.

Why did I say that?

"I thought I heard something." Okay, that was marginally better.

I finally lift my eyes to his.

"It's not safe in here," he says. "Someone must have removed the no trespassing sign." His narrowed gaze clearly implies that I'm the one that did it.

"I'm not doing anything wrong," I say, defending my actions even though I'm doing nothing more than standing in an empty building. But those eyes are piercing me like he can see every deep, dark, and bad thing I've done in my entire lifetime. And maybe the faded pink granny panties I'm currently sporting.

Heat rises up my neck.

"Except trespassing," he finally says.

"I didn't know."

"Doesn't make it any less illegal."

My defenses rise. What is this guy's deal? It figures the first person to actually talk to me is a big jerk. "What are you, a cop?"

"This building is condemned. It's not safe. It's being torn down next month."

"But I thought I heard—"

"I can't stand here and argue with you all day." He steps back and motions for me to come out. Even though I hate to comply with such a belligerent if unspoken command, I follow him into the sunshine breaking through the early morning fog.

When I turn around to face him, he's already jogging away.

Chapter Three

A FEW DAYS PASS, and I still don't have a job.

And we're running out of food.

And Paige needs new clothes because she apparently grew an inch since last week and her jeans are turning into capris.

We finally met our neighbor though.

His name is James Bingel. The postman delivered his mail to us by accident, and when I went to deliver it to him, he actually opened the door to take his mail.

Then he slammed the door in my face without saying anything else.

A definite improvement.

I sort of expected Castle Cove to be like the movies. Neighbors would immediately show up with cookies and invites to tea. Precocious children would offer to mow the lawn and do odd jobs. A handsome yet brooding stranger would fix the car or move in next door or . . . insert romantic trope here.

Instead, less than a week in and I have a reclusive neighbor, a sullen teenager, and a broken car. And the brooding stranger yelled at me instead of asking me out. This is not how it's supposed to happen.

Although, I'm not surprised. My life has never been the stuff of romantic comedies. More like a tragedy.

I had no idea finding work would be so hard. I'm sure it doesn't help that I have no referrals or legitimate work experience, but people have to start somewhere, right?

Other than spending my time being rejected at every place I've looked for a job, we've also spent most of the last few days cleaning up the house and setting up Ruby's stuff.

We've gotten a few shipments so far. The first thing we put up was the sign out front. It was formed from some distressed wood and painted a burst of colorful reds and yellows. Ruby's Readings and Cosmic Shop, it reads in a whimsical, flowing font.

There were a few boxes of books, crystals, and some packaged herbs for clearing the air of spirits or something, which we've unpacked and put in the display cases in the front room. "I'm hungry," Paige says, sitting in the chair on the other side of the reading table while I flip through one of the books that came in about palm reading. We've decided the reading room is our new favorite place. We set up tapestries and wall sconces, as well as the beaded curtain in the doorway. It's almost homey.

"Are you sure you don't have a tapeworm?" I tease, but the truth is that I'm starving, too. We've been subsisting on ramen noodles and peanut butter.

She sticks her tongue out at me and drums her fingers on the table.

"Here," I say, reaching into my pocket for our last twenty-dollar bill. After this it's pocket change until I find something to support us with. Or decide to trap some seagulls for dinner. "Go get us something for dinner from Stella's."

Stella's is a diner on the other side of the boardwalk. We almost drowned in our own drool the other day walking by and smelling the burgers. By unspoken agreement, neither of us said anything about the heavenly smell, knowing we didn't have the funds to splurge. There's something about being so close to rock bottom that's making me reckless.

"Really?" Her face lightens. It's almost worth facing certain starvation to see her smiling again.

"Really. Go. Be careful. Don't talk to strangers."

She rolls her eyes but bounces out the door.

A few minutes later, I'm still sitting at the little table, perusing Ruby's book about palm reading—do people really believe this shit?—when the doorbell rings and I nearly fall out of the chair.

Through the beads that line the doorway between the reading room and the shop, I spy a couple of college-age looking girls peering in the front window.

They aren't neighbors holding casseroles, but I'll take it.

I open the door, but before I so much as open my mouth, one of the girls is speaking.

"Are you giving readings?" She's short and blond, her haircut is stylish, and her jeans are expensive. The other girl is a darker blond, with longer hair and a closed expression.

We are probably about the same age. They must be spring breakers.

"I don't—"

"This is stupid, Cassie," the darker-haired girl interrupts.

"You're such a killjoy. It's fun."

"It's bullshit."

Her friend is right, but I'm not going to defend her.

Cassie faces me. "Please? I've always wanted a reading, like, so bad. I'll pay double whatever you normally charge."

I'm about to open my mouth and tell them that I'm not Ruby, that I don't do readings, and I can't tell the future any more than the rock in the front yard can get up and twerk all over the front lawn, but something stops me.

I could do this.

No, no. I just lectured Paige about our new beginning. No cons. No lies. But we could really use the money. Honestly, if I don't find income of some kind soon, we'll be begging for food and I don't think Mr. Bingel will feed us.

Just once can't hurt. I have at least thirty minutes before Paige gets back. The walk to Stella's takes ten minutes and it will take at least fifteen for them to cook the food. I can take this nice girl's money, maybe even help her out a little bit, and then she'll be gone. No one will know. I can play psychic for thirty minutes. I've done worse. Besides, I was just reading Ruby's book and it's just a lot of vague statements and unprovable predictions anyway.

My mouth opens. "The shop is closed, we're under construction." And then my mouth keeps moving. "But I'll make an exception if you're willing. Double my rate is two hundred dollars," I say, instead of what I should say, which is the truth. Part of me hopes that the price will be too steep and she'll just leave and I can forget any of this ever happened.

But the price doesn't even make her blink.

"Great!"

No going back now. I step back and she walks into the shop.

"There's no way," the friend says, still standing on the

porch, shaking her head. "I'll meet you at the boardwalk when you're done."

She leaves and I smile at Cassie and lead her into the reading room.

I light a few candles on the table and take a few slow breaths, trying to get into character. What would a psychic say? I need to get Cassie to relax and also give me some hints about herself that I can use to convince her I'm legit.

"Is there anything specific you would like to ask or know about?" I ask, hoping she'll give me some clues to go off of without realizing she's doing it.

Cassie contemplates the question, her brows furrowing as I sit down in front of her. "I don't know."

Not helpful.

"Let me see your hands," I say.

She opens her palms face up in front of me and I reach for her wrists, taking a moment to look over her hands when I'm really thinking about what the hell I'm going to say next.

I lead with the obvious.

"You have some big changes coming."

Who doesn't?

Her eyes widen and she nods.

"Graduation?" An easy guess. She's the right age, and it is spring break. A tactic my mother taught me at a young age: most of the time, you can make generalized statements and assumptions based on what people are wearing or their age. If you give them even the tiniest hint that you might know something about them, they grab onto it like you know everything. More often than not, they'll even drop more hints about themselves without even realizing they're doing it.

"Yes." She nods eagerly, leaning forward.

"This worries you for some reason." I frown down at the lines in her palm, like they will tell me anything. More telling is the slight indentation on her ring finger.

"You recently dissolved a relationship," I say. "A very serious one."

She gasps. "Yes. How did you know?"

I smile at her. "It's my job." To look at your hands and pretend like I know what I'm talking about.

"Oh, right," she laughs.

"You were together a long time," I venture.

"Since high school."

She seems sad. A barb of guilt stings my chest. Even if I'm a crook, I might still be able to help her.

"Don't worry about this guy. I know it seems like you'll never find someone better, but you will."

She scoots forward, peering down at her hands, which are still lying open between us. "It says that?"

"See this?" I point to a line that spans her palm. "This is your heart line, and according to this, your love life is not over yet."

I have no idea if that's accurate, but it is the heart line according to the book I was just reading. Plus she's a pretty girl, and she seems sweet. Surely there's love in her future.

She bites her lip. "I have a date with a new guy tonight, actually," she confesses.

I nod, like I knew all along.

"We're having dinner at The Castle Cove Restaurant on the pier. We had to make reservations like a month ago. Do you think it will go well? What does it say?" She's still looking down at her palms like she can read the answer there herself.

Oh shit.

"No," I say, maybe a bit forcefully.

"What?" She leans back, her eyes flying to mine, her expression slightly bewildered. "It won't?"

"Ummm." Double shit. I shake my head slowly. "I'm not getting a good feeling about the restaurant tonight. I think you should stay away."

This is no lie; explosive diarrhea on a first date would be a terrible experience. I'm not sure if whoever took in the delivery at the restaurant decided to go ahead and sell the bad fish, but better safe than sorry.

"Oh." Poor Cassie's expression is a bit defeated.

"I think the location is the problem. Maybe convince him to take you to Stella's? It's not far, and it's also a nice place," I say, although the clientele there tends to be more geriatric than college-aged. But going somewhere without high expectations will reduce the stress of a first date anyway.

"Right." She nods, but her eyes are puzzled.

I blather on a bit more about positive changes coming her way and other cryptic nonsense until she starts to relax.

We talk for a bit longer. She's a business major graduating next year, but she also enjoys playing the violin. It's almost too obvious that she's some kind of musician, given the calluses on her fingers.

When I finish the reading, she seems happy even though I didn't actually tell her anything, and I'm two hundred dollars richer.

Paige returns home right as I'm shoving the money into the cookie jar in the kitchen, along with a big dose of shame that I've acted no better than my parents so soon after swearing off everything they taught me.

I will never do this ever again.

But I did help Cassie, right? And no one was hurt; she probably didn't need that money. She'll be back in her dorm in a few days, having completely forgotten about her reading, and Paige and I will be able to eat for another two weeks.

The thought doesn't soothe the sickness in my stomach.

Chapter Four

W E PIG out on burgers and fries and end up in a food coma in our PJs in the living room, watching reruns of *I Love Lucy* for hours.

I don't tell Paige about the college girl or the fake reading or the two hundred dollars I've stashed. She didn't realize how dire our situation was anyway, no need to burden her further. And no reason to tell her and make her think it's okay to run any cons while we're here, because it's definitely not okay and it will never happen ever again.

Besides, this is what life is all about. Hanging out with Paige, relaxing, not fearing our parents' recriminations or what they'll do next.

The laugh track from the TV is lulling me to sleep when there's a sharp pounding at the door.

I sit up quickly.

Paige and I exchange a glance.

We don't have to talk. She nods and gets up to hide in the kitchen.

What if Ruby sent someone to check on us?

I stumble to the door. It's dark outside. Who could be here at this hour? It's raining, I hadn't even realized. As I peer through the peephole, the sky spits fat drops of water into the street and patters steadily on the roof. It seems as though it's always raining or overcast here. Hopefully it's just the time of year.

I'm surprised to see that the person standing on my doorstep is the same person who yelled at me on the boardwalk.

It's the runner. Cute butt man.

More surprising is his outfit.

He's in a police uniform.

My face burns with embarrassment as I remember our exchange from the other morning. What were my exact words? Oh yeah, *What are you, a cop?* He never answered the question, but apparently the answer is yes, yes he is.

How did I not see it sooner? The military-esque haircut, the too-observant eyes, the confident way of moving that makes me want to rip my clothes off and . . . oh, right. Okay, that's how I missed it.

This is the last thing we need. What could he possibly want? Is this about that stupid trespassing thing? That can't be it. He would have said something more at the time; he wouldn't have just run away. What if he found out I gave a fake reading to Cassie and he's here to arrest me for operating without a business license and impersonating a . . . psychic? I'm not sure that deserves a late-night appearance, but who knows.

There are other options of course, since my past is a giant cesspool of illegal activity, but there's no way my parents would call the cops. That's not their MO. They would come after us themselves if they were so inclined.

Schooling my features to remain calm, I take a deep breath and open the door. I can do this.

Recognition lights his eyes, but it doesn't disturb the professional mask he's wearing.

I open my mouth to say something, anything, like can I help you, how are you, do you know what time it is, what the hell are you doing here you asshole, but nothing comes out.

Instead, I stare, openmouthed.

"I'm Deputy Reeves." He pulls the hat from his head, shaking water off the brim. "Do you mind if I come in?"

My brain stutters on the deputy part before finally connecting with my tongue.

"Of course not." I step back and let him in and then shut the door, hanging onto the knob for support behind me while I face him.

What is it with this guy and his effect on my brain?

He stands in the shop entrance, just a few feet from the door. I didn't turn on any lights, so the only illumination comes from a wall sconce behind him in the next room and the porch light filtering in through the window behind me. From my vantage point, his eyes are dark and dangerous, and the shadows sharpen his features.

"Is this about the other morning?" I ask when he doesn't say anything, proud that I'm actually able to speak finally.

"No."

Another pause. I can sense him assessing me and I don't think he likes what he sees.

I'm wearing an old T-shirt, soft with age, and lumpy sweats that make my ass look like a root vegetable.

In contrast, his uniform is impeccable, ironed, creased, and up to code—except for the spattering of water dusting his shoulders from the downpour.

There are two kinds of cops in this world, the kind you can buy off and the kind you can't. The first type is drawn to the job by the power it lends them. They use their authority to make other people feel small and to move themselves up in the world, by legal means or not.

The cop at my door is not this type of cop. He's too serious, too put together. He's the second kind, which is almost more dangerous for people like me.

"I'm here to talk to you about someone you spoke with earlier today. Cassie Graham."

Oh shit. Maybe he is here to arrest me.

Stay calm. What would someone who didn't break the law say right now?

"Is she okay?" I ask.

"She's all right. A little shook up, but she'll be okay."

"What happened?"

His eyes narrow at me. "Don't you already know?"

My brain buzzes for a second. Does he suspect me of doing something to her?

I stare at him, saying nothing, but this time it's on purpose. If I open my mouth, I could dig myself into an even bigger hole. How much does he know?

He finally speaks. "She says you predicted what happened to her and you'll know who it was."

My breath catches at his words, and the already nervous thumping of my heart increases.

I predicted . . .

He's not here to arrest me.

He thinks I'm Ruby. Of course he does. The only real thing I told Cassie was to stay away from the boardwalk. Maybe she went anyway, and something—other than food poisoning, apparently—happened to her. She told the cops I predicted this . . . whatever it is.

I'm immediately thrust into a very serious problem. I can't say I lied and took her money and gave her a fake reading. Not only did I impersonate someone else, I did business as someone else. Without a license. I'm pretty sure that's ten shades of illegal. This guy doesn't seem like the type that would laugh it off and let me go. What if I'm arrested? What would happen to Paige?

My brain shuffles through options quickly and lands on the only one that makes any sense.

I have to pretend to be Ruby.

For the first time, I think it's good that I have experience at deception and . . . well, basically bullshitting my way through situations.

I shake my head at his question. "I didn't think what I saw in the reading would come to pass so quickly," I say, sealing my fate.

Slipping into the lie is like slipping into an old shoe. It's comfortable but a bit stinky.

"What exactly did you see?"

Violent diarrhea.

I clear my throat and turn around to face him, tamping down my internal thoughts before I speak. "It wasn't very specific. It was more a feeling that something bad would happen if she went to The Castle Cove Restaurant. What did happen?"

"I'm afraid I can't release that information, but a crime was committed."

A crime? So I was right. Not food poisoning, but something else. What are the odds that I would warn her away from a place where a crime would be committed against her?

"Where are you from?" he asks suddenly.

I blink at the sudden change of subject and have to think quickly about the things I know about the real Ruby. It's not much. "New York."

"What part of New York?"

"Upstate."

"What made you move to Castle Cove?"

"I was looking for property near the ocean, and I found a listing for this address. Am I in trouble for some reason?"

"No."

There's another heated pause while we consider each other. His eyes are dark and intense. He doesn't like me. It shouldn't bother me. I've spent my whole life pushing down feelings. Like Mother always said, emotions make you weak. But I've never been good at that, and the vague sense of distrust emanating from Deputy Reeves is getting under my skin. I'm not trying to hurt anyone. I've done nothing to earn his scorn.

Except lie straight to his face just now, multiple times.

Dammit.

"If you have no more questions, Deputy," I move around him and open the door, "I have things to do."

He stands there for a long, tense moment, and then he brushes past me on his way out the door. "Have a good night." I don't think he means it.

I watch him put his hat on and walk to his patrol vehicle. I try not to stare at his butt.

It's unfortunate such a nice ass exists on someone who is such an asshole.

"What did you do?" Paige asks from behind me after I shut the door.

Well, crap. Time to come clean.

My shoulders sag in defeat. "This girl came to the door while you were getting the food. She wanted a reading and she offered two hundred dollars. She thought the shop was open and that I was . . ." I don't have to finish that sentence. Paige can fill in the blanks. "I couldn't say no."

Her eyes widen. "Two hundred bucks? I wasn't even gone an hour and you made two hundred bucks?"

"I'm so sorry—"

"That's awesome!" The words explode from her.

Not the reaction I was expecting. "No, it's not, it's terrible. I shouldn't have done it."

"How did you know something would happen to her?"

"I didn't. She said she was going to eat at The Castle Cove Restaurant, and I overheard someone there the other day talking about getting a shipment of old fish."

Her eyes gleam. "That's pretty lucky."

"Or unlucky."

"Don't you see, Charlotte? This is the answer."

"The answer to what?"

"To all of our problems. You can be Ruby." There's a gleam in her eyes I don't like.

"Um, no, I can't be Ruby."

"Why not?"

"Because Ruby is coming back."

"In like four months. Think about how much we could make in four months. Enough to fix the car or get a new place to live, and then we just have to leave before the real Ruby gets back."

"This isn't how things are supposed to be," I say.

"But you know I'm right. There's even a cop that thinks you're Ruby. This town is too small. You can't go back to being Charlotte. And we can't leave yet. We have no money, no car, and nowhere to go. We'd be crawling back to *them* within days. Is that what you want?"

I shake my head with a groan. "You know that's the last thing we'd do."

She smiles. "So you get to be Ruby. Can I be Trixie, your young but stylish assistant?"

"No. If we're doing this, I'm the only one that can get in trouble. You still get to be Paige, my annoying and way too smart for her age sister." I rub my eyes. "I can't believe this is happening," I mutter.

Paige grins. "It's going to be so much fun."

Chapter Five

"YOUR DAUGHTER IS USELESS," my mother told my father on a sunny day in June.

That's how they always referred to me. "*Your* daughter," as if neither one were willing to claim me as a product of their loins. How could I be, they would lament. I was nothing like either of them.

Sure, I had my father's brown eyes and my mother's wide mouth, but I was too soft. Too emotional. Too easily attached to others. Boring. They never cared how much I did to help them. Never cared that I basically raised Paige on my own, never mind that I was only eight when Paige was born.

"Just have her go out with one of their sons. She can get intel on the family, like she did in Newbury. She was good for it."

Mom laughed, a high-pitched, mocking sound.

They talked about me like I wasn't sitting right there, in the shade of the palm tree only ten feet from them. They laid on fluffy chaise lounge chairs, basking in the sun. The mansion we were renting had a lagoon-style pool with a working waterfall.

Blissful, they said. This was everything they'd worked for and what they deserved, they said.

It felt like hell to me. But pretty much everywhere we went was hell, ever since I'd gotten old enough to have thoughts of my own. The only good part of my life was Paige.

The pool was pretty to look at I supposed, but I couldn't swim. I just wanted to read in the shade, not listen to my parents throw shade.

"She won't be able to get any of those boys to ask her out," Mom said. "They're good-looking and popular. Two of them are on the football team and one plays lacrosse. And have you seen her lately?"

My face flushed in shame. Sixteen, and I looked more like thirteen. It's not like I could help it. I was too thin, barely any curves, and the smattering of adolescent acne didn't make the picture any prettier.

"Put some sexier clothes on her." Dad had no shame in whoring out his eldest daughter. "She'll be fine. Some guys like that younger look, you know? Their father does anyway. Maybe it's in the genes."

They laughed while I cringed.

"What about Paige?" Mom suggested. "She's better looking."

My blood ran cold in the hot sun.

I had to get Paige out before she got much older. I just needed more money. It was hard to hide things from my parents. They were already suspicious of everything and perceptive to boot.

But with those words, I couldn't remain silent. Talking about me was one thing; talking about Paige was where I drew the line. I stood and walked over to them.

"Leave Paige out of it. I'll do whatever you want."

"Of course you will." Mom stood up and got in my face. "You know what else you can do? Learn how to swim!"

She pushed me in with a laugh loud enough to hear even under the cool water of the pool, even in my dreams.

~

"Shit." I sit up in bed, breathing hard. It wasn't a dream. I mean, it was a dream, I'm not flailing in the pool, but there's water all over the bed and dripping onto my lap.

I look up and a drop hits me on the forehead. There's a water spot tinting the formerly white ceiling above me, which is already turning brown.

Oh, no. I can't believe this.

Ruby didn't leave any provisions for leaky ceilings.

"No. No, no, no, no," I mutter, the single word becoming a mantra. I climb out of the damp bed and step onto wet, squishy carpet. I press my palms against my forehead. This can't be happening.

"Paige!"

I run downstairs and grab pots and pans and towels and I'm frantically running around the top floor of the house in a T-shirt and panties, hunting down leaks, when Paige finally emerges from her room.

"What's going on?" Her hair is a rumpled mess and her eyes are still puffy with sleep.

"We've sprung a leak." I toss her a towel.

It's still raining a little outside, but it's slowed to a drizzle. The water seems to be restricted to the bedroom and the hall-way. The office is all clear and dry.

Small mercies.

By the time we've set up all of the pots and bowls and sopped up as much water as we can, I'm ready for a drink.

I'm going to have to find a way to get in touch with Ruby to have this fixed. This isn't a minor repair. Maybe her accountant person can help me fix this mess. In the meantime, I'll have to sleep with Paige. Ruby's going to need a new bed and everything.

But what if I call this accountant person and they want to come here? They could potentially blow my cover with the cop.

I try to work out the problem in my head. No need to descend into a full-blown panic attack yet, but a knock at the door distracts me from my thoughts.

I open the door without taking the time to look through the peephole.

It's Deputy Dipshit himself standing on my porch, again.

This time he's brought another officer. He's a couple years younger than the deputy. His face is more open and friendly, with boyish features and an easy smile.

"Good morning, ma'am. We're, uh, sorry if we woke you," the young officer says with a sheepish grin, his bright blue eyes sliding down my bare legs before darting back up.

I glance down and realize I'm still in my underwear and T-shirt.

Deputy Reeves's expression is as closed off as ever, but I don't miss the momentary heat in his eyes when his gaze flickers up and down.

The other officer is still grinning at me.

"Oh, crap." I press my eyes shut, as if that will make everything around me disappear. "If you'll excuse me for a minute."

I turn and practically run for the stairs, calling out behind me, "Come on in and make yourselves at home."

I hear a chuckle, probably not Deputy Douchebag. I can't imagine what would make that stone façade laugh.

Upstairs, Paige is still in her PJs, her hair wild. She's on her hands and knees, sopping up water from the hardwood floor in the hallway. "Who's that?" she whispers.

"The cops," I whisper back.

"Oh shit."

"Watch your mouth."

"Are they going to arrest you?"

"I don't think so. Stay upstairs."

"Ugh," she complains but then disappears into her room.

Once I make it into my own room, I shut the bedroom door and lean back against it, needing to catch my breath for a moment and gather my thoughts.

Now I have two cops who think I'm Ruby. And they're downstairs right now. What could they want? There's only one way to know and I can't hide forever.

I throw on the first pair of shorts I find that aren't wet.

Downstairs, the cops are still in the front room, perusing the items we've been setting up in the display cases and on the shelves.

"Do you see this?" The younger officer lifts up an item, showing it to Deputy Reeves. "This stone here helps get rid of negativity. We should put like ten of them in your patrol car. Maybe one up your—"

"Sorry about that," I say when I re-enter the room.

They both turn and look at me.

"That's no problem, ma'am," the younger cop says. It's weird to be called ma'am when he's got to be only a few years older than me. "I'm Officer Reynolds. But you can call me Troy." He holds out his hand and I shake it.

"Can I get you gentlemen anything to drink? I have, um . . . water?"

No money for anything else. Although I think there was some lemonade concentrate in the freezer.

"I would love some—"

"This isn't a social call," Deputy Reeves interrupts.

"I apologize for my partner here. He had a bad night."

"I'm sorry to hear that," I murmur, crossing my arms over my chest. "What can I help you with?"

They exchange a glance, and then Officer Reynolds—Troy —is the first to speak. "As you're aware, you had some business with a Miss Cassie Graham yesterday."

I nod. It surprises me that the deputy would let Troy take the lead. It's obvious from their postures and conversation— even if I didn't know their job titles—that the deputy is the one in charge. People in positions of power don't easily relinquish those controls. I also find it more interesting than I should that Troy was teasing the deputy when I walked in. What kind of cop talks to their superior like that? What kind of deputy allows it? Especially one that seems so rigid and severe.

"It would appear that you told her to stay away from the boardwalk." Troy stops, his eyebrows rising, waiting for my confirmation.

I nod again, not seeing any harm in admitting the truth.

"Well," he continues, "she didn't listen, and last night she was the victim of a mugging."

"She was robbed?" I glance over at the deputy. Still Mr. Blank Face. So that's what he wouldn't tell me last night.

"Yep."

Why tell me this now? "What does this have to do with me? I didn't rob her."

"You're not really a suspect," Troy says with a shrug. "You advised her away from the scene of the crime, which would make it difficult for you to be implicated. However, when the victim made her statement, she was pretty emphatic about how she should have listened to you and how everything you said was accurate. So, the chief wanted us to come talk to you about the case."

He glances over at Deputy Reeves once more before continuing. "You see, we really have no leads."

"None?" I ask. "Did Cassie see the person's face or any identifying marks or anything?"

"Nope. And that's the problem. It appears the perpetrator came up behind her and put a bag over her head before running off with her purse."

I frown. "That's odd. There were no witnesses?"

"No. It was dark and late. Miss Graham was outside the restaurant by herself."

We're quiet again for a few seconds while I process the information and they watch me expectantly.

Well, Troy is expectant; Deputy Reeves is unreadable.

Troy shakes his head, his expression sheepish. "Crime isn't common in Castle Cove. We have zero unsolved cases. So, after hearing Cassie's story and given our lack of any leads, the chief wanted us to come here and see if you would help us with the investigation, or if you had any . . . you know . . . feelings or whatever."

Shock pulses through me. I stare at them, unsure how to proceed.

"It wouldn't be the first time law enforcement asked a

psychic to help with a case," Troy continues. "There was this TV show, *Psychic Detectives*. She helped catch a killer once and—"

Deputy Reeves interrupts. "Can you help us or not?"

I shake my head, thinking things through as quickly as I can.

Pretending to be a psychic for a college kid to run a quick and harmless con is one thing; pretending to be a psychic for a bunch of law enforcement officials is insanity.

"I can't." I think quickly to bolster myself with potential excuses. "I'm trying to start a business. I can't afford to take time away from that right now. And it's not an exact science. I don't always see specifics. Sometimes the information comes through, and sometimes it's blurry or vague, or nothing happens at all. You might be wasting your time and resources. And I don't . . . feel anything right now," I add.

"But—" Troy starts.

"That's fine," Deputy Reeves says at the same time, cutting off the younger officer again. He's already heading for the door. "We'll let the chief know your answer."

Troy follows behind him at a slower pace.

"Tell the chief I said thank you for thinking of me," I tell Troy before he can exit with the deputy.

"I'll tell him. I'll talk to my sister, too. She would love to get a reading from a real psychic. Maybe I can send some business your way."

"Oh. That's nice," I say weakly.

Why did I ever open my big mouth?

"Reynolds," Deputy Reeves barks from his car.

"I better get going. Don't want to anger the beast." Troy rolls his eyes before heading down the path to the driveway.

"I heard that," Deputy Reeves calls.

"I intended you to," Troy says and then flips him off.

The deputy's expression gets even more glacial—if that's possible. "This isn't a preschool, Troy."

"Could've fooled me with the way you've been whining all morning."

The car doors slam, locking me out of the conversation. I can't help but smile as I shut the door even though I'm dying inside.

"Are you going to help the cops?" Paige asks, appearing from around the doorway.

"Are you insane?"

"Maybe they'll pay you."

"Running a con on the town is bad enough. I'm not running a con on the cops."

She shrugs. "Fine." And then she grins. "I have an idea."

<h1 style="text-align:center">Chapter Six</h1>

"YOU STOLE spy cameras from Mom and Dad?"

"They stole them first, from those FBI guys that used to follow us around. I thought we might need them. And I was right. Maybe I'm a little psychic, too." She tosses me a grin over the top of the computer.

"So let me get this straight. Your plan is to set up bugs and get dirt on all the residents of Castle Cove?"

"Not for like, blackmail or anything, just so you have material and they'll think you're a real psychic. Like what you overheard at the restaurant. We could use that kind of intel for readings."

"You are not bugging anything," I say. "And I'm not breaking into people's houses."

"Not their houses, just places people go a lot. I bet we'll hear a bunch of stuff." She taps on the keys for a moment. "This place is like going to one of those Amish farms. There's no cameras anywhere, didn't you notice? It's weird. It's like living in the last century or something."

I noticed that, too. Even the general store only uses those

big circular mirrors for surveillance. Not that I was planning on robbing them or anything, but scouting for recording devices is sort of second nature to us.

The problem is that I don't want this lifestyle to be second nature to Paige.

With a sigh, I move toward the computer. "Move."

She took four cameras from our parents' stash. They're pretty high-tech, wireless, and can live-stream to a computer from any location, once I link them to an IP address. They can also connect to satellite, so we're in luck. After checking each one to make sure they still work, we narrow down the spots in town to plant them.

Then we spend the rest of the day creating flyers on Ruby's computer.

"We should have a grand opening," Paige suggests as we're figuring out what to put on our advertisements.

I nod slowly, still not into the idea completely but realizing there's not a ton of options.

"We can't sell Ruby's products though," I say.

"Why not? We won't use that money; we'll save it for her. We'll only use the money you get from the readings. Maybe then she won't press charges on us or try to find us if we leave her with some start-up cash. Plus it would be weird if we have all this merchandise coming in over the next couple of weeks but don't sell it."

This whole thing just keeps getting worse and worse, but I nod. It makes sense.

"We need to open in two weeks," I say. "That will give us time to gather some intel. But we can't wait too long. I'm not sure how far I can stretch the two hundred dollars we have."

Paige nods her agreement. "We can do this. Everything will be great." She smiles at me.

I turn the computer monitor to show her the finished product. "What do you think? I can offer speed-dating-type readings, ten bucks for ten minutes."

I found a font similar to the one on Ruby's sign. *Grand Opening*, it reads. The brightly colored paper promises psychic readings and chakra balancing—for a fee, of course.

"It's good." She grins, way more excited about this whole thing than I am.

The next morning, we're ready to put the plan into action.

"Good morning, Mr. Bingel," I call to the neighbor as we're leaving.

He's outside trimming his rosebushes. He did the same thing yesterday, when I also tried to talk to him, but he still hasn't said anything back. Not directly anyway.

He mutters something under his breath about how the name Ruby sounds like a hooker. Then his speech rumbles into something about morons and stupidity and foolish girls before he stands up and stalks inside his house. Paige laughs. "He's funny."

I'm glad she's finally in a good mood, but I'm not sure how I feel about the fact that it took getting involved in illegal activity to finally excite her.

"You do the flyers, I'll set up the bugs," I say as we walk down the sidewalk.

"Fine," she agrees, knowing that I won't budge on this. I'll let her help, to a point, and even that's pushing it.

The activity on the boardwalk is slightly more hectic than it was only a few days ago due to the college kids that have trickled into the area since spring break began.

Between planting the bugs, we put flyers up on some of the poles situated around the boardwalk.

When we've finished, Paige insists on going to the bathroom before we walk home. I wait outside while she uses the facilities at the hardware store. I spend the time watching the brunette woman at the register, who seems distracted by some guy with shaggy hair leaning over the counter toward her.

People are funny. Their body language indicates they are both into each other, leaning forward, arms open, but the furtive looks they cast each other clearly indicate they don't want the other person to know. They're lucky. I wish I could experience something as innocuous as a flirtation. I wish that my biggest problem was whether someone liked me or not.

My back aches and I rub it. I had to sleep with Paige last night due to the wet mattress in my room, and she's not the easiest sleeper. I got punched in the face twice and kicked in the kidneys at least three times.

The day before, I called the international message-only number Ruby left me to tell her about the leak—and maybe to feel her out and make sure she was still in India and not intending to wing it back stateside anytime soon. I ended up leaving a message with the Indian man who works in a shop a few miles from the ashram. He spoke heavily accented English and kept calling me "Most Honorable Madam Charlotte."

I didn't call Ruby's accountant, although the ache in my back might change my mind. But what if he shows up and blows my cover? We can't risk it.

A hand tugs at my sleeve. "Would you like to buy a kitten?"

I glance down. It's a small boy with dark, unruly hair and a dirt-smudged face. He's no more than six.

"Have you gotten a lot of business with that look?" I ask.

His big brown eyes widen even further. "What?"

I sigh. I could have scripted this ploy. In fact, my parents made me use the dirty urchin when I was a child. It's effective. And kittens? What's better than children and kittens? It's like the perfect con.

"Hey, who's this?" Paige joins us outside the hardware shop.

"He's selling kittens," I tell her.

She grins, pure delight crossing her face as I'm sure she's thinking the same thing I am.

She nudges me with her elbow. "We should look at them."

Okay, maybe not.

"No animals," I say firmly. I've already broken enough of Ruby's rules, not to mention the fact that I've stolen her identity.

"We won't buy one, we'll just look," she says before turning to the boy. "Is that okay?"

He smiles, a dimple winking in his right cheek, and then yells, "Come on," as he darts away.

Paige follows and I have no choice but to tag along behind them.

At the end of the boardwalk, almost to the road, we stop. There's a saggy box with an older boy sitting beside it. He's younger than Paige, maybe nine or ten.

"Here's the kitty," the little urchin says when we stop.

I crouch down next to Paige and peer in the box. It's a large, dirty, black cat with a torn ear and a missing leg.

It hisses at me.

"That's not a kitten," I say.

"What happened to his leg?" Paige asks with a tsk, her tone entirely too sympathetic.

I shoot a look at her, but she doesn't see it. She's too busy gazing with soft eyes at the cat and the boys.

This is not happening.

"It was a terrible accident," the older boy says.

They must be brothers. They have the same wild dark hair and spattering of freckles across the bridges of their noses. They're wearing worn, but clean clothes and they haven't showered in a few days, if the dirt under their nails is any indication.

Not that that's very odd for boys. I don't think.

"What kind of accident?" I ask.

They glance at each other and then the older boy speaks. "He got caught in a trap." He doesn't meet my eyes until after he's done speaking.

I don't think he's lying, but I get the sense he's hiding something.

"What's his name?" Paige asks.

"Gravy," the little one says.

My eyebrows lift. "Gravy?"

He nods vigorously. "Will you buy him, then?"

I open my mouth to give a firm and vehement no, but Paige's face stops me cold.

We've always wanted a pet. One time, Paige brought home a stray dog. As soon as our father found out, he took it away. We never asked what he did with it, didn't want to know. We never tried to bring home an animal again.

"How much?" I ask.

The younger child speaks first. "Ten dollars."

"Twenty," the older brother says quickly. "We're trying to save up money for new bikes."

I shouldn't do it. But Paige deserves something normal. Something that other kids do. Something other than running a con. I don't know if it's the longing in their eyes, or the fact that I'm a total pushover when it comes to giving Paige what she wants, but the words pop out.

"I'll tell you what, why don't you boys help us bring the cat to our house? All my cash is at home."

They're both nodding and agreeing before I have all the words out and Paige squeals and throws her arms around me.

"The cat is your responsibility," I tell her.

"I know, I'll take care of him, I promise."

"The house isn't far." I gesture up the street. "Just a few blocks."

The older boy carries the box with Gravy and we walk up the road together in silence for a minute.

"What's your names?" I ask finally.

"I'm Greg Sullivan and this is my brother, Gary," the older one tells me.

"I'm Paige and this is my sister, Ruby." Paige flashes me a quick grin after the lie slips out of her mouth.

"I heard someone talking about you," Gary says. His eyes are wide and curious, staring up at me. "Are you a witch?"

"No, I'm not a witch." But I'm a little concerned people are talking. I didn't realize I had been noticed, but I suppose with the cops coming over and everything, word was bound to get around.

"I heard someone saying you tell the future, and that's not natural."

I shrug. "They might be right."

"Can you tell my future?" he asks, eyes wide.

We pause as we reach the road. I take Gary's hand and motion for them to wait for a passing car before we cross.

"Yeah, tell them the future, Ruby." Paige is enjoying this entirely too much.

"You're too young. Your future can't be determined because you haven't made enough important decisions to know who you are and how you'll react to things."

I have no idea what I'm talking about, but it makes him nod—if a bit uncertainly—and I don't have to make up anything to tell them.

Once we reach the house, Paige takes the boys and the cat into the living room, and I grab a twenty out of the cookie jar, where I stashed the money from Cassie the other day.

"Here you go." I hand the money over to Greg.

He shoves it into his pocket without meeting my eyes. "Thanks. We have to go. Our dad is waiting for us at home."

"All right." I walk them out to the front door.

Paige can't be bothered, too busy with the cat.

Before they leave, Gary hugs me, his arms gripping me around the waist for a few short seconds before he pulls away. "Thanks for taking care of Gravy."

He sounds a bit sad, but I don't have a chance to see his face because he turns and they're racing down my front lawn and back down the street toward the boardwalk.

I frown after them. Something is going on with those boys. I don't have time to linger on it though because a howl from the living room catches my attention.

A few hours, a lot of soap and water, and about twelve scratches later, Gravy is sort of clean. And I think he hates me. He didn't scratch Paige once, reserving all his slashing for when I was in the general vicinity.

After his forced bathing, he darted under the couch and we haven't seen him since.

It's while Paige is helping me put salve on my cuts that I realize we don't have any cat food.

"I'll go get the food," Paige says.

"You're not leaving me alone with that demon cat."

"What if someone comes for a reading?"

"They can wait."

In the end, we both walk to the store for the food.

"Thank you for getting the cat." Paige hugs me then, stopping our forward progress in the middle of the sidewalk in front of Mr. Bingel's house.

"You're welcome." I take a second to enjoy the hug, since the older Paige has gotten, the more infrequent her displays of affection have become.

When she finally releases me, I realize that someone is standing on our porch.

It's a woman with long, dark hair, wearing jeans and a colorful top. That's all I can tell from our vantage point.

"Can I help you?" I call out as we're walking up.

"Hey," she says when she spins around. "Are you Ruby?"

That's a loaded question.

She has dainty features and is a few inches shorter than my own five foot five. She's holding a casserole dish and she has a warm smile on her face. She's probably my age, maybe a year or two older.

She's also familiar. I recognize her as the woman behind the counter in the hardware store where Paige planted a bug today. The woman who was flirting with the shaggy-haired guy.

"I'm Paige," my sister says into my silence. "And this is my sister, Ruby. Are you here for a reading?"

"I'm Tabby Reynolds," she says. "Not here for business, just a friendly visit. I would have been by sooner, but I didn't realize they'd finally sold this house. It's been on the market for years."

I recognize the last name and put the pieces together. It helps that she and Troy look so much alike. "Are you Officer Reynolds's sister?"

"I am." She beams, her smile bright and infectious. "He told me you were new in town, so I made you a casserole. Well, Mrs. Olsen made you a casserole." She lifts the dish slightly. "I just saved you from her company." She snorts, the inelegant sound a bit startling, coming from her delicate frame. "Come on, I'll help you bring the stuff inside."

"Right." I notice she didn't really give us a choice. I hand the bag of cat food to Paige and unlock the door.

Tabby follows us into the kitchen. "Have you had much business from the locals?"

"We're not open yet," I say carefully.

"Troy said you had a customer though, the one who got mugged, and you totally predicted it and everything."

Paige pulls a bowl out of the cupboard and fills it with cat food.

"You know about that?" I ask.

"This is a small town. It's hard to sneeze without everyone seeing the color of your mucus."

Paige laughs.

Lovely. No wonder even the kids had heard of me. It's also concerning. The real Ruby was only here for a few hours, but what if someone saw her? Or talked to her? How can I explain it if I'm asked?

"How does that whole psychic thing work anyway?" Tabby asks.

"It's hard to explain," I hedge. I take the casserole dish from her.

"Well, how did you know what would happen to that girl?"

Keeping my story consistent, I tell her what I told her brother. "I knew something bad would happen, but I didn't know what it was exactly. I don't always get details, just a general sense about things."

"Oh." She appears a bit let down at that.

"Sometimes I get more specifics. It depends on the reading." I turn away to put the casserole in the fridge.

"What happened to your cat?"

When I pull my head out of the fridge, Tabby's standing in the space between the kitchen and the living room, where she's been snooping around, apparently.

Paige answers. "He's a rescue cat. We just got him today." She makes tsking sounds with her mouth, trying to draw the feral beast to his food.

"He looks demented," Tabby says.

Now it's my turn to laugh.

She's not wrong. Even clean, Gravy's bum leg and frayed ear make him look like a cat possessed. I'm just surprised she's so straightforward with people she barely knows. In my limited experience, people are always extra polite when they first meet. They don't show their real personality until later.

"So I'll be blunt." Tabby pulls up a chair at the small wood dining table and sits.

"You weren't already being blunt?" I ask.

She just grins and keeps talking. "You guys are new in town, so if you don't want to face the inquisition, you'll tell me all about yourselves and I'll spread the word. Trust me, it's easier this way," she says, nodding solemnly.

Paige and I exchange a look.

"I'm not sure—" I start.

"It's fine," Tabby assures me, waving off my concerns with a flick of her hand. "We'll do this quick. I'll be gentle." She opens her purse and pulls out a pen and a small notebook, on which is some sort of list.

I laugh in surprise. "You aren't kidding."

"I wish I was. Where are you guys from?" she barks, all business.

We give her some of the canned answers I already gave Deputy Reeves and the story we concocted to explain why I'm raising Paige. We're from New York, our parents are dead, etc.

After I've given her the basics, Paige gets bored with us and rejects our company in favor of the TV and combing Gravy, who seems to love it, purring and rubbing his head against her.

The questions get weirder as soon as Paige is out of earshot.

"Are you single?" Her pen taps against the notebook.

"Yes."

"Do you have any kids? I mean, your own, other than your sister?"

"Just a three-legged cat named Gravy."

This doesn't faze her at all. "Awesome. Are you gay?"

I cough. "What?"

"You know, do you prefer men or women?"

"How is this relevant?"

"It's not. But, don't worry. This isn't, like, a judgmental thing. It's so the old biddies know who to hook you up with."

I shake my head. "I'm not planning on hooking up with anyone."

"That's what they all say," she mutters.

Dear lord. "I need a drink."

She nods. "Good idea."

I pull a pitcher of lemonade out of the fridge.

"Is there vodka in that?" she asks, eyeballing the glass suspiciously.

"No."

"Tequila?"

"No."

"Well then what's the point?"

"There's about three cups of sugar." I pull a couple of glasses out of the cabinet.

She eyes me speculatively, pursing her lips. "You're weird, aren't you?"

I shrug, flushing a little bit. I probably am weird, my childhood wasn't exactly normal, but I thought I put on a good front.

"It's cool. I thought you might be. We can smell our own."

I'm not really sure how to react to that other than laughing.

A few hours later we've nearly polished off the lemonade and eaten half the casserole, with Paige's assistance. I've learned that Tabby is the most brutally honest person I've ever met—not that I've met many people. It's strange, and I'm waiting for the other shoe to drop. What does she want from me, really? I'm not used to someone hanging around me without having some kind of agenda. Except Paige.

"Tell me about the people here," I say. It's only fair since I've been evading her questions for the entire afternoon. Plus, the more I know, the better.

"Who do you want to know about?"

"Anyone. Everyone. Tell me about the town."

"There's not much to tell," she says. "I grew up here. It's small and boring and full of old people. The old biddies run the entire town and have the ultimate say in everything. There's some elderly men who think they have some power, but we all know the truth."

"Okay . . . what about you?"

"What about me?"

"Family?"

"You've met my brother, Troy."

I nod and refill her glass, eyeing her face while I pour. "Are you guys twins?" Their bone structure is nearly identical.

"Yep. Well, he's older by three minutes. He just started working for the sheriff's office last fall. We both grew up here. Our parents retired a couple years ago and decided to travel around the country in their RV. I took over the hardware store. It was my dad's business and Troy didn't want to run it."

"You like running the store?"

"I do. And I like fixing things."

"Can you fix roofs?"

Her brows lift. "Did you have leakage from the storm the other night?"

"Unfortunately."

She grimaces. "That stinks. Water damage is no joke."

"Do you know what's up with my neighbor?"

"Who, Mr. Bingel?"

I nod.

"He just kind of keeps to himself since his wife died. That was . . . man, like ten years ago now. She was a lot more social than he is. I see him at the store sometimes though."

"Does he talk to you?"

"Not really. He just grunts and pays and leaves. But that's how he's been since I was a kid. Even before Martha died."

"Oh." I guess I can be glad it's not just me and Paige reserved for his disdain.

"I think he doesn't know what to do with himself. They had one kid, a son who was older than me. He died in Afghanistan so now he's alone."

Poor Mr. Bingel. No wonder he's so grouchy all the time. "What about these old biddies that run the town? Should I know anything about them?"

"There's Mrs. Olsen," she says.

"The casserole maker."

"Yep. We call her Grandma sometimes but it's more of an honorary title. She takes care of me and Troy and has plied us with food ever since our parents retired and moved away. She's also the town matchmaker. Or so she thinks. She's always trying to hook people up, but they usually end up with someone other than whoever she thinks it should be. It's pretty hilarious." She makes a face. "Unless it's you she's trying to match, then it's terrifying. You'll know when you see her because she always wears clothes with cats on them."

"Cats?"

"Oh yeah. Big ones. I don't know where she finds those things. She has at least a hundred cat shirts; I never see her wearing the same one twice. Then there's Miss Viola. She's deaf as a rock, but it's hilarious to watch her and Mrs. Olsen have conversations. You'll meet the rest of the ladies eventually."

We sit in companionable silence for a few moments before I ask, "What about Deputy Reeves?" I try to sound casual.

I mean, I am casual. I want to stay out of trouble more than anything else. Totally. It has nothing to do with his piercing eyes and killer butt.

"Jared grew up here, like the rest of us. He graduated a

couple of years ahead of Troy. He moved away after high school and went to college across the country—that's where he got into law enforcement. He moved back just a few years ago when his parents . . . Well, he had to come back."

Interesting. "What happened to his parents?"

"They died. Car accident."

I grimace. "That's too bad."

"Yeah. He hasn't really been the same since. He used to be sort of a bad boy. For senior prank day, he stole Farmer Barney's pigs and set them loose in the school. There were only three pigs, but he painted the numbers one, two, and four on them." She laughs. "I heard the teachers spent hours searching for pig number three, but there wasn't one. People are still telling that story."

"That's pretty clever." I try to reconcile the image of a boy who would pull that prank with the man who looks at me like I've let my dog poop in his yard. "That doesn't really seem like the Jared I've met."

"No," she quickly agrees. "Not even close."

We both take a drink of our lemonade, and then she says, "I'm glad you moved here."

"You are?"

"There's not a lot of women in town that aren't married and under the age of fifty. Most people move away after high school, since there aren't any colleges nearby and there's not exactly a ton of jobs for career-minded folks."

My parents would love this place. Older people are often the targets of cons because they can be easier to manipulate: bored, trusting, lonely, vulnerable to mental impairments, and living on their pensions. They tend to accumulate more money than their younger counterparts, and they are prime pickings if you offer to grow those savings into something that can make their last days more exciting or that they can give their surviving relatives. I internally shove those thoughts away. That's not why I'm here.

I'm about to ask who she hangs out with then, but a crash and loud howl of pure pain fill the air.

Followed by the unmistakable sound of Paige's voice. "Oops."

"What is that?" Tabby asks.

All I can do is groan and give a one-word answer. "Gravy."

I run toward the noise, wincing as the wailing increases the closer I get.

Tabby is on my heels. I stop abruptly when I get into the front shop and she runs into my back. I almost scream louder than the damn cat when I see the mess, but I manage to restrain myself to a tortured groan.

"What's wrong?" Tabby asks from behind me. She's too short to see the havoc the cat has wreaked.

He's knocked over an entire display rack. Of course it's one of the ones we stocked with some product that came in earlier. Fragile product. Glass product that's now in shards all over the floor.

He's pinned to the ground underneath the shelving unit. The corner of the display has dug into the wood flooring and Paige is frantically trying to rescue him.

After a moment of wanting to kill the damn beast and Paige, or leave them to their fates, I instead pick my way through the rubble and help Paige free him from the now-broken shelf. He must sense his life is in imminent danger because he races out the door and disappears down the dark hallway.

Paige isn't quite as quick to flee.

"I'm sorry Ch— Ruby." She winces at the slip.

"It's okay," I say.

"Gravy was trying to jump onto the display case, and I was trying to stop him but I didn't catch him in time."

"It's not your fault. Why don't you go check on him? I'll clean this up."

She nods and leaves, still a bit mopey.

I kneel on the ground, picking up shards of glass and wood.

Why do these things always happen? Now we'll have to replace this stuff, too. Something else to add to the never-ending list of expenses that seem to pile up around me like an avalanche of crap.

"Hey." Tabby is next to me on the ground. "You're going to hurt yourself. This is all broken. You can't save it."

She's right, but I don't want her to be right.

Her words hit me particularly hard. *You can't save it.*

But I have to. I have to fix this.

I suddenly feel like if I can't save this, I can't save Paige. Or myself.

And that's been the point all along, hasn't it? Even though I seem to have fallen into a disaster of my own making.

Maybe I can't be fixed.

Maybe once you're in with the bad guys, you'll always be one.

Maybe Paige would be better off without our parents . . . and without me.

I stop picking up the mess and sit there, staring down at the shards of glass that litter the floor like so many broken dreams.

"Are you okay?" Her voice is hushed, like she senses the mental breakdown about to commence.

"I'm fine. I just . . ." I drop the pieces in my hand and they patter back to the ground. "I can't do this."

"It's okay, we just need a broom and a dustpan and—"

"No, you don't understand. I can't do this. I can't do any of this." I gesture to the entire shop. "I don't know why I'm trying. I'm a failure, and I haven't even started."

"You're not a failure." Her voice is quiet and serious when she probably should be asking me to chill the eff out. "You only fail if you stop trying."

Tabby, a woman I met literally hours ago, is crouched on the ground next to me, her hand on my arm, giving me more comfort than I've had from anyone in my life other than Paige. This stranger is treating me better than my own parents ever did.

I have no idea what to say.

"Come on," she says, removing her hand from my arm. "Let's clean this up."

In silence, we sweep up the mess. She holds the dustpan as I gently push the shards of my life into the trash.

Then she slaps me on the back.

"We need booze."

Chapter Seven

"I CAN'T LEAVE Paige for very long," I tell Tabby for about the thirtieth time since we left the house.

Not that Paige cares. She assured me that she would be fine, she's not a baby, she's practically an adult.

Then Tabby assured me that we would only be gone for a couple hours, tops. Castle Cove isn't exactly crime-ridden—minus the mugging at the pier the other night—and with the door locked, Paige is as safe as the crown jewels. So she says. And we'll be less than a mile away, at Ben's Tavern.

The bar is loud and crowded. Even with all the convincing, cajoling, and assurances from both Tabby and Paige, I'm not sure that I should have agreed to this little outing, but it's too late to turn back now. I'm still a bit raw from my emotional collapse, but Tabby's exuberant presence has helped.

"I'm getting us a round," Tabby yells in my ear over the loud hum of people talking and laughing. She disappears between bodies in the crowd, presumably heading toward the bar.

Everyone who lives in this town must be stuffed into the

small space. As soon as Tabby disappears, I stand there like wood piling trying to withstand the waves of bodies crashing around me. I don't know anyone. I don't really want to talk to anyone. I haven't had much luck with the residents so far.

There's nowhere to sit; all the tables and booths are full of people. I shuffle over to lean my back against the wall and watch.

Ben's Tavern is a mishmash of odd items and conflicting themes. The bar itself is gleaming wood, and it's well maintained. There are some sports jerseys hanging on the walls next to black and white photos of old rock stars. There's a stage for a band on one side, along with a karaoke machine stuffed in the corner. Then there are weird items hanging from the ceiling over the bar, from pictures and hanging dollar bills to plastic frogs.

There are a few pool tables with mostly guys surrounding them. I recognize Officer Reynolds—Troy—in his off duty clothes: a T-shirt, jeans, and a baseball cap pulled low over his eyes. I watch them play for a few minutes, taking note of their techniques and abilities. I wish I could watch with disinterest, but some habits are hard to break. Officer Reynolds isn't bad, but he's not great either. The guys he's playing with are better, but they aren't as good as me. Pool sharking is one of the easiest cons to pull, especially if you're a woman. Women are eternally underestimated.

Before long, Tabby reappears, thrusting some kind of mixed drink into my hand.

"Drink quick," she says, then takes a long swallow out of her own glass.

"What? Why?"

"Just do it." Her hand circles, motioning for me to hurry.

I lift the glass to my mouth and she reaches up and tilts it even more, forcing the cold liquid down my throat. I sputter for a moment, pulling the glass away, but before I can ask Tabby why she wants me to slam it, there's someone else standing in our little circle.

"Tabby, I told you you're not allowed behind the bar anymore." It's a guy. He's tall and slender with sandy-blond hair and an annoyed expression. I think it's the same guy I saw Tabby talking to at the hardware store.

"I'm not behind the bar," she says.

"You're going to be behind lots of bars if you don't pay for your drinks," he insists, but the words lack heat.

"Whatever, Ben." She flips her hair over one shoulder. "You know my brother won't arrest me. If anything, he'll defend me and probably pay for my drinks. Not that he should. You totally owe me."

He sighs and shakes his head before he seems to realize that I'm standing there, watching the exchange.

"Hey." He nods in acknowledgement.

"This is Ruby," Tabby introduces me. "She owns the new shop over on Norfolk. Ruby, this is Ben, the owner of this fine establishment and a total pain in the ass."

"Oh right, I've seen the sign. Ruby's Readings." He ignores Tabby and sticks his hand out.

"Nice to meet you."

He turns back to Tabby, pointing an accusatory finger in her direction. "You owe me ten dollars for those drinks."

"I owe you dick. And ten dollars? Really? This ain't the Bellagio."

"Ruby." Someone else enters the conversation, stepping between me and Tabby and slinging an arm over my shoulder.

"Officer Reynolds," I say, stiffening slightly. I suppose it's normal when you're in a bar to be overly familiar with other patrons, but I'm not sure I've ever willingly been this close to a cop in my life.

"I'm off duty, call me Troy. I'm here to rescue you from these two losers and their never-ending bickering. It's cute at first but it slowly turns into wishing you could burn your own ears off. How about a game of pool?"

"I don't know how to play." The response is automatic.

"I don't want you to play, I just want you to watch," he says with a grin.

I glance over at Tabby, but she's still arguing with Ben.

"She won't even notice. They get into it and it's at least an hour before they come back to the real world. Trust me."

Out of excuses, I relent with a nod. I follow him to the pool table, where he puts aside my now empty glass. Then he pours me a new glass of beer from a pitcher on a nearby stool.

"You don't have to be a psychic to know who's going to win this game," Troy says, puffing his chest out and then pointing both thumbs toward himself. "Me," he mouths.

I can't help but laugh.

He starts racking the balls, glancing over his shoulder to ask, "Seriously though, can you predict if I'm gonna win? Because I want to know if I should put money on this."

I glance down at his opponent. It's an older gentleman standing on the other side of the table, holding a cue stick and talking to someone else.

"I don't know. He looks pretty skilled."

The man in question chooses that moment to belch loudly.

"Yeah. He's a real shark," Troy says drily. "Are you sure you're psychic?"

"I told you—"

"I know, not an exact science. Don't worry, I won't be all judgey like my partner. I might tease a bit, but," he shrugs, "sometimes things happen that can't be explained, and I'll never rule any explanations out, paranormal or otherwise."

"That's very open-minded of you."

"I'm a pretty cool guy," he says with a grin. "You can ask anyone."

Just then, there's a cacophony of shouting from across the bar. Troy morphs into cop mode, the fun-and-games expression immediately replaced with seriousness. He stalks toward the commotion.

I can't see what's happening from here, but whatever it is disperses quickly and the sound level returns to the normal laughing and clinking of glasses.

Within moments, he's back.

"Is everything okay?"

"It's fine." He grabs a pool cue from a nearby shelf and chalks it. "Typical Friday night in Castle Cove. Wouldn't be complete without the Newsomes getting into some kind of argument." He shrugs.

I have no idea who the Newsomes are, but it's too loud to ask and Troy is already breaking the balls.

I sit there and watch the pool game for a while, keeping a side eye on the rest of the bar. Most of the patrons are older than me. And Troy. And Tabby. In fact, we might be the youngest ones in here by twenty years. Tabby wasn't kidding about that median age thing. The music starts up, and even the band is over fifty.

After a little while, Tabby reappears with a couple of full

shot glasses in her hands, and her clothes are a little more rumpled than I remember.

"What happened to you?" I ask.

"Nothing," she says quickly.

I glance over at the bar where Ben emerges from somewhere in the back. His hair appears more artfully disarrayed than it did before they disappeared.

"You and Ben fight a lot, huh?" I look at him and then back at her meaningfully.

"He's a punk-ass little shit."

"Your shirt is on inside out."

"Dammit." She hands me one of the shot glasses. "Here, drink some more."

Whatever's in the glass is dark purple. "What is this?"

"Don't ask questions, woman. Drink!" She clinks her glass to mine and shoots it down.

"I can't drink too much, I have to get home to take care of Paige soon."

"Oh c'mon. She's not an infant. She'll be fine. We'll send Troy over there later to make sure she's not burning the house down or having orgies."

"Orgies?"

"Relax, I'm kidding. Look, Ruby, we take care of each other here. You've had a rough time of it, moving, raising your little sister. You deserve a night off to let loose a little. Trust me."

My eyebrows lift. I don't even know her. I've never trusted anyone other than Paige.

At the expression on my face, she rolls her eyes. "Troy!" she yells over the noise.

"What?" he yells back.

"Tell Ruby to drink and that her sister will be fine."

"Drink, your sister will be fine," he obliges and then frowns. "You have a sister?"

"Ruby, seriously," Tabby says, ignoring Troy's question. "I will make sure you don't get too drunk and that you get home safe to Paige. Scout's honor." She holds up three fingers in salute.

"Promise?"

"Pinky swear." She holds up a finger and I shake it.

"Just this one drink." Then I shoot it.

Tabby claps her hands and throws an arm around my shoulders. "Now let's dance!"

Time passes. I'm on the dance floor, surrounded by mostly strangers, old strangers, and Tabby until we're both sweaty and laughing.

The band finishes their set. Some of the crowd disperses with the music. Since there are open spots now, Tabby drags me to the bar.

"*Garçon.*" She bangs on the bar top. "Gimme a shot of something."

"I think I should cut you off," Ben grumbles, but he puts two shot glasses on the bar and fills them with a clear liquid.

"Don't be such a party pooper," Tabby says, then takes the shot back.

She puts the glass back on the bar, a frown twitching at her lips. "Was that . . . water?"

Ben's shoulders shake with laughter.

Tabby climbs on top of the bar to get to Ben, who backs away quickly, his hands up. "No need to get violent. And get off my bar." He commands but doesn't do anything more than flick the bar rag at her and run in the opposite direction.

A loud shout and then a crash from somewhere down the

bar distracts me from Tabby's antics. I can't see over all the heads between me and the commotion, but a crowd of people by the pool tables shifts and gets louder. A male voice yells, "I will kill you if you touch my wife!"

Another voice, female and just as loud, yells back, "Ex-wife!"

Ben is already jumping over the bar. Troy pushes his way through the crowd to break up whatever kerfuffle is happening.

"The Newsomes again," Tabby says. She's on the other side of the bar. She must have made her way over while I was trying to see what was happening.

"Who are the Newsomes?" I crane my neck to catch a glimpse of the infamous couple. When the crowd parts, I get a momentary peek. They aren't as exciting as I expected, both likely in their sixties. Mr. Newsome is balding and mostly gray, and the ex-Mrs. Newsome has dyed red hair with gray roots and lipstick on her teeth.

Tabby puts a drink in front of me, pulling back my attention. I eye it warily. This one is lime green.

"They've been separated for years, but they always do this. At least once a month they go out when they know the other one will be here and start a ruckus." She waves her hand. "It'll be fine. Troy will break them up." There's another loud crash and an inarticulate yell. She shrugs. "Maybe."

From my perch on the barstool, the crowd still seems a bit agitated, but that changes when the door swings open and Deputy Reeves strolls in.

He's in uniform, but even if he weren't wearing the badge, he has such a presence that the crowd parts for him, bodies shifting back as he cuts through the throng of people.

When Tabby sees him, she laughs. "Jared will fix it. He fixes everything in this town. Ready for this? Just watch. Or listen." She holds up her fingers and counts down. "Three, two . . ."

As if she's the psychic, the melee dies down and the hum of conversation returns.

"See? Now take your drink like a good girl." She nudges the glass in my direction but I shake my head.

"I think I'm done for the night."

She rolls her eyes. "Fine."

"Tabby. You're not supposed to be behind the bar."

Jared's voice next to me sends a shiver up my spine. I'm not sure if it's a sexy shiver of awareness or a scared shiver of anxiety.

Tabby's expression is wounded. "*Et tu*, Jared?"

He sighs. "Just make sure you get a ride home."

"Do I look like an idiot?"

"I think it would be better if I didn't answer that question."

Tabby laughs. "My girl here, we're just having some fun. You've met Ruby, right?"

She knows that he has.

He glances over at me. "We've met."

He doesn't sound super excited about the connection, but I try not to take it personally.

"She's awesome, right?"

I have to smile at Tabby's enthusiasm on my behalf. He doesn't answer that question, either.

"Did you settle the Newsomes down? What was it this time?" she asks.

"Apparently Sheila came here with Doug, and then Paul and Doug had a disagreement."

Tabby snorts. "Never fails." She explains for my benefit. "Sheila and Paul, a.k.a. Mr. and Mrs. Newsome, were married for twenty years. But they've been 'separated,' " she makes air quotes with her fingers, "for the last two years. Doug was their neighbor. Sheila only brought him to make Paul jealous. I swear those two are worse than a soap opera and just as predictable."

"Speaking of predictable," Jared looks at me, "make any more predictions recently?"

I shrug, uncomfortable with the way he's watching me and the tone of his voice. He asks like he already knows the answer.

"She's not working right now, Jared. Lay off," Tabby says.

"That's funny." Jared glances over at her. "She was willing to open for business when Cassie Graham offered her two hundred dollars the other day."

I swallow.

He's not wrong.

Tabby gives a low whistle. "You really charge that much for a reading? You must be good! Do I get a friends and family discount?"

I don't answer her right away, instead engaging in a battle of wills with Jared while we stare each other down.

The best way to tell a believable lie is to believe what you're saying. You have to be confident and assured. They're called *confidence* men for a reason.

Keeping my eyes locked on his, I answer Tabby's question. "No. And I didn't want to give Cassie a reading the other night either. She was very insistent. So I charged extra for the inconvenience. Is there something illegal about that, Deputy?"

I raise my brows in challenge, inwardly pumping my fist because I finally formed a full, coherent sentence in front of him.

He shakes his head. "Not illegal. Not exactly ethical, but not illegal either."

Tabby changes the subject, probably sensing the tension

between us. She says something about a weekly dinner at Grandma's and blabbers about some kind of drink that she wants to make me.

I'm not really listening. I take a sip of the drink she placed in front of me and enjoy the scorch as it goes down, the heat nearly as intense as the burn on my face right now.

I know what the heat in my face means. It's shame. Deputy Jared Reeves is closer to the mark than I'm comfortable with. After a minute, he steps away to talk to Troy, nodding at both of us because of course he'll be polite even if he thinks I'm the worst person on this planet since Stalin and Joseph Goebbels combined.

As soon as he leaves, I turn to Tabby, lifting my now empty glass. "I'm going to need another one of these."

Chapter Eight

I WAKE up to a splitting headache and the sound of snoring in my ear. Oh shit. Did I go home with someone?

Blinking against the bright light streaming in through unfamiliar pink curtains, I spy a dark head on the pillow next to me.

That's not a dude.

It's Tabby.

How drunk was I last night?

I lift the blankets. I'm still fully dressed, so maybe I wasn't drunk enough to have my first lesbian experience. I shut my eyes against the glare of the sun and sag back into the pillow. The last thing I remember is my conversation with Jared, being full of shame and regret and then drinking too much before agreeing to take some shot of something fiery blue, a color that cannot possibly exist in nature. The rest of the night is a complete blank, with sporadic blurs of more drinking and asking Deputy Reeves to show me how to get the pool cue out of his ass while Tabby laughed so hard she nearly fell over, bringing me with her.

Then we must have come back here. Why didn't I go home, what about—?

"Paige!" I yell, scrambling out of the bed but getting caught in the sheet.

Tabby's soft snores are cut off by my yelling and flailing.

"Dude, chillax." She groggily sits up and watches my hysteric attempts to extricate myself from her blankets. Her hair is a wild mess around her head and her voice is raspy from sleep. "Paige is probably still asleep since we woke her up at like two in the morning. She's in the guest room."

I still my frantic movements. "We did?"

Tabby yawns and lies back down, fluffing her pillow. "Yeah, you wouldn't stay here without her so we all piled in the patrol car with Jared and went and picked her up—"

"We did?"

"Don't you remember? You told us how you've been sharing a bed and Paige kept corn-holing you, so I offered to let you guys stay here for the night since my bed is way better for two people. We let Paige sleep by herself in the guest room." She pauses. "I'm still not sure I understand what corn-holing is, but whatever."

I sag back against the comforter.

Even in my drunken haze, I somehow managed to take care of Paige.

"Thank you," I tell Tabby, feeling guilty now for waking her up.

"Yeah yeah, now shut up," she says, closing her eyes.

I lie back down cautiously, not wanting to disturb Tabby any more than I already have. But I can't sleep. I still want to make sure Paige is okay.

When she was a baby, I used to watch her sleep all the time.

She was so amazing, tiny, and perfect. I didn't understand why our parents weren't as obsessed with her as I was. I constantly worried something would happen to her, but I was the only one. Our parents would let her cry all night. They kept their door shut against the noise. I learned how to prepare bottles and change diapers at an early age. I never really minded it though. It was actually nice to have someone to be with, someone to take care of, someone to love. Love was a foreign concept for our parents. Well, loving other people. Self-love they had no problems with.

Paige was all I ever had.

More carefully this time, I untangle myself and slide out of Tabby's bed. Down the hallway I find the guest room where Paige sleeps peacefully, arms and legs spread out, taking up the whole space available, as usual.

Relieved, I make my way to the bathroom. I wash my face and rinse with mouthwash to get out the taste of last night.

While drying off with a lace-trimmed pink towel—which looks nothing like anything I would expect Tabby to own—I hear a thump out toward the living room.

Pausing to listen before putting the towel back on the rack, I lean toward the door. Is someone awake?

"Dammit Tabby, with the freaking shoes in the freaking hallway!" It's a male voice. Troy?

I peek my head out of the door. Down the hallway, Troy's leaning one hand against the wall to support himself and rubbing his foot with the other hand.

"Are you okay?" I whisper, stepping out of the bathroom and heading down the hall toward him.

"I'm fine. Tabby leaves her shit everywhere." He gestures to the ground where at least six pairs of shoes are lying in haphazard heaps. "She hasn't changed since we were four. Always just throwing her crap around and leaving it in the best places to try and kill someone." He shakes his head. "I'm glad you're here. I wanted to talk to you."

Oh no. What now? Did I do something else totally embarrassing last night that I've since repressed?

He grins at my panicked expression. "Come on, I'll make you coffee."

That relaxes me a little. If he's making me coffee, it must not be too bad.

In the kitchen, he pulls out the coffee cups and fiddles with the machine on the counter until there are two steaming mugs.

He sets one in front of me along with a container of sugar and creamer.

"Thanks," I say, stirring in the cream.

"I talked to the chief this morning." Troy takes a sip out of his own cup.

I take my own fortifying drink and wait for him to continue.

"He really wants you to reconsider helping us with this case. We still don't have any leads."

"I don't know, Troy . . ."

"He agreed to pay you contract rate. We can work around your schedule. You would still have time to prepare your business and then spend time on the case with us periodically or at night even. We have someone on call every night anyway, which will be great since, as you said, the gift doesn't work on command. Even if you don't see anything, or whatever, you'll still be paid for your time hourly. But if you help find the thief, you'll get a bonus."

It's not fair to come at me in the morning when I'm tired

and hungover and even more broke than I was twenty-four hours ago. I haven't even finished my first cup of coffee.

I can't possibly help law enforcement for three reasons. One, I'm a fraud. I'm no more psychic than Gravy is, and what if they figure that out?

Two, I'm not Ruby. I'm sure I'll have to fill out some kind of tax form with information. Although, I do have all of Ruby's information from her office. I found it the other day . . . But I can't think of that. I am not thinking of ways this might work, I'm thinking of why it's a bad decision.

Three, if it gets out that I'm helping the police with this case, there could be media interest, and I have no doubt that my parents will jump on that—even if they aren't actively trying to find us. At the very least they'll have their little feelers out there, seeking word. They won't take kindly to anyone getting one up on them. They might not love or even like me and Paige, but that won't stop them from taking action to get back what they see as theirs.

Finally, I really don't want to spend any more time than necessary with Jared. He obviously finds me suspicious— because he's smart—and I don't really enjoy being subjected to the loathing that pours off him in waves and settles in my general direction every time we're around each other.

Okay, maybe that's more than three reasons.

But then again, I can't help thinking of all the damage from Gravy that I'll have to find money to replace if this con is going to work. And the roof that needs to be repaired at least to some extent if we're going to last another four months. Then there's the car. Plus clothes and school supplies for Paige. The list of things we need is never-ending. On top of all of that, it would be nice to save up some money because we're going to have to leave town when the real Ruby gets back and hope that she doesn't use her powerful, rich family to track us down.

Maybe I could do this.

"You should do this." A voice behind me echoes my thoughts.

Paige is standing in the doorway of the kitchen.

"I should?"

She nods. "If it helps someone . . ." She shrugs.

I know what she's saying. If it helps someone, namely us. Having an in with the cops is like a dream when you're running a con. It'll be easier to know if they're onto us.

I breathe in deeply, then out again. I'm running out of excuses not to, which might shed more suspicion on us than anything else.

"Fine. I'm in."

"Yes!" Troy claps me on the back.

"I don't want any media involvement," I add. Maybe I can at the very least make an effort to resolve one of my issues.

"But it might help your business if—"

"No. I don't care about that. I don't want that kind of attention."

He nods. "Okay. I don't think that will be a problem. I'll pass the info along to the chief. Anything else?"

"Yes." I hand him my cup. "More coffee."

He takes it with a grin. "You might need more than coffee."

"Why's that?"

"Well, if you're free tonight, Jared's on duty. You can start by hanging with him."

Chapter Nine

"P LEASE TELL me you got something for me to go on."

"I think I do," Paige says, swiveling around in the chair to face me before swinging back to the computer.

I didn't want Paige to help review the tapes, but I didn't have much of a choice. She couldn't sign for the shipments that came in for Ruby's shop, and I need something to go on before Jared gets here.

"Thank you baby Jesus," I say. "Whatcha got?"

It's after six, and we haven't even had dinner. I have less than thirty minutes before Jared gets here so we can do whatever it is I'm supposed to be doing, and I have no idea how I'm going to help them solve the mystery of the Castle Cove Bandit. At least, that's what the newspapers are calling it.

"The general store has a strange occurrence every morning at ten."

"What is it?" I walk behind her to see the video she's streaming.

"Well, there's a shift change when the guy at the bakery

goes on break. Before the new guy gets there . . ." She pauses the video and points. "See this old lady with the hat? Every day she goes in there, and there's five cupcakes on this shelf. Now look again." She forwards the film and then stops again. "Now there's three."

"That's it? That's what you got? Some old lady stealing cupcakes?"

"I didn't say it's the best lead, but if she's stealing cupcakes, maybe she's stealing other stuff."

"It's kind of a leap from cupcakes to mugging."

Paige crosses her arms over her chest. "Well, it's something that you know that maybe other people don't. It'll at least make them believe you know things."

"Or they'll think I'm a few fries short of a Happy Meal," I grumble. Although, it's probably too late for that if the way Jared acts around me is any indication. "Sorry, Paige," I add when her face falls. "I'm not really looking forward to conning the cop, and I don't want you doing any of this. You did a good job. I'll see if I can use it."

She smiles.

The doorbell rings.

Of course, he's early.

I suppress a groan, but Paige lights up. "He's here!" she says, bolting for the door.

I follow at a slower pace.

"What are your intentions with my sister?" she's asking when I make it downstairs.

"Paige," I call. "Go do your homework."

"I don't start school until Monday."

"Well then go do chores. Feed the devil cat or something." I give her a screw-with-me-and-die look.

"Fine," she grumbles, shuffling out of the room and down the hall.

"Tabby will be here in an hour," I call after her retreating form. "No candy!"

If she's hyper and crazy when Tabby comes over, I'll never get her to babysit again.

I steel myself with a deep breath and then turn to face Jared.

He's in uniform, the outfit ironed and cleaned and impeccable as ever, a matching hat in his hands.

"Hi."

He nods.

Well, this isn't awkward.

"Come in." I step back and motion for him to enter.

He glances around the shop a bit warily before coming inside, rubbing his thumbs over the brim of the hat in his hands.

Is he nervous? The thought pleases me a little and calms my own nerves.

"So how does this work?" he asks. He's frowning slightly and there's a crease between his brows.

I can't help but smile. He probably thinks I'm going to do some crazy voodoo or eat the head off a chicken or something.

Well. I can't let him down now can I?

"First, we should go into the reading room," I say, leading him in that direction. "That's where I keep the sacrificial virgins."

That startles a cough out of him.

A laugh would have been better but I'll take what I can get.

I hold the beaded curtain aside for him to enter the reading room. His eyes are lowered, but they snap up to my face when I turn. Was he checking me out? The thought is oddly exciting, even while the idea of anything happening between us is beyond impossible. We won't be here in a few months anyway, and, ugh, he's a cop.

Once he's followed me through the beaded curtains, I light the candle in the center of the small table while he stands near the doorway.

"Sit down."

He complies, but he doesn't look happy about it.

"We have to hold hands." I lean my arms across the table, the candle flickering between us.

There's a noticeable hesitation but then he hangs his hat on the back of his chair and gingerly places his hands on mine.

His fingers are warm, his palms lightly callused.

"Close your eyes," I command. I shut my own eyes, but open them again a few seconds later.

He's staring at me blankly.

"Close your eyes, or it won't work."

He frowns slightly but shuts his eyes.

I take a deep breath in and then hum it out, like I'm trying to get into the zone. Really, I'm thinking about the best way to mess with Jared. He totally deserves it.

"Now think about what you know about the mugging. Really concentrate on it. Focus on any negative energies in your . . . chakras," I say. "Inhale with positive energy, exhale with the negative. Inhale, exhale."

"How is this doing anything?"

"Shhh." I squeeze his hands in admonishment. "I almost had something and you made me lose it."

He huffs, but his eyes are still closed.

"I see . . . a woman."

I think he rolls his eyes behind his shut lids.

"She's older. She's on a farm."

His eyes are still shut, the ever-present crease between his eyelids winking at me.

Wait. Where was I going with this? That's from *The Wizard of Oz.* Wrong story.

"Hold on, it's not a woman on a farm," I change my mind. "It's the general store. But there is a woman. In a hat. That's where we have to go." I release his hands, slapping them slightly before standing up.

"That's it?" Jared opens his eyes. "A woman in a hat at the general store? That's what you got from all that?"

"Yep. Let's go. The universe is pointing us there."

He sighs, clearly thinking I'm a lunatic. "Fine."

It takes us longer to get there than I thought it would.

Mostly because Jared went over all his rules before he would let me in the patrol car, and there were a lot of them. Have your seatbelt on at all times, stay out of my line of sight, buttons aren't toys, etc.

"Am I allowed to breathe?" I ask.

"Only when your face is turned slightly to the right and away from the controls."

"Hey! You made a funny."

He almost smiles at me. Almost. It still looks more like a grimace, but I'm being optimistic.

The ride to the general store is mostly silent. Nothing more than the occasional drone of the radio and the rattle of tires against the pavement until we park in front of the general store.

Jared leads the way inside and to the register. We have to wait a minute while an elderly lady in a gold jogging suit purchases three long candles, a length of rope, and a can of whipped cream.

I'm still contemplating what she's going to do with her purchases when it's our turn with the clerk.

"Hey, Barry," Jared tells the man at the register. Barry has thick glasses, a white beard and a gold earring in one ear that completely throws off the rest of the image. His nametag proclaims him to be the assistant manager.

"Heya, Deputy. How can I help you?" Barry asks, his eyes sliding to where I'm lurking behind Jared.

"I've brought Ruby here to ask you some questions."

"Okay."

Jared turns and looks at me, brows raised.

"Right," I say. "Hi, Barry. I was wondering if you could tell me about some missing cupcakes."

Barry's eyes widen and then flash over to Jared. "Why is she asking about that?" His voice sounds a bit panicked.

Jared turns to face me. "What about cupcakes? You said it was about a woman in a hat."

I swallow thickly, heat creeping up my face. Why are they so concerned about the damn cupcakes? I hope Paige's video intel doesn't get me in even more trouble.

"It is about a woman in a hat," I say. "And cupcakes. Cupcakes that are being stolen."

"What does that have to do with the mugging?" Jared asks.

I shrug. "I don't know, I'm just going with what the universe presented."

"And this is what the universe presented. Cupcakes."

I don't appreciate his tone. "You asked me to help you."

"Believe me, it wasn't my choice."

My eyes flick from Jared to Barry, then back to Jared. "Why is it such a big deal that I'm asking about cupcakes? Maybe there's a connection and we should pursue it."

"Sorry to waste your time, Barry." Jared takes my arm and steers me toward the exit. "Come on."

"Where are we going?"

"You'll see."

We get in the patrol car and he starts driving. I get a bit concerned as we approach the sheriff's office, wondering if he's taking me there to lock me up and throw away the key, but he continues driving past the innocuous brick building.

He finally parks in a small lot next to a giant grassy area that's surrounded by a short, gray stone wall. It's a cemetery.

"What are we doing here?"

He doesn't answer me. Instead, he gets out and I follow him. The sun is setting, and the tombstones cast long shadows around us. I can't see the ocean, but it must be close because the salty sea breeze tickles my face and blows my hair in my eyes.

He stops in front of a small plot with a cement square imbedded in the ground.

George Hale, the script reads. Beloved Husband, Father and Friend 1939-2014.

Laid out next to the grave are a cupcake and an empty wrapper.

"Mrs. Hale brings cupcakes here every day."

I stare down at the chocolate confection.

"They were George's favorite. She hasn't been able to bake anything since he died. So she has to buy them." He pauses for a minute before clearing his throat and continuing. "Mrs. Hale has a bit of a QVC addiction. Her daughter lives in New Harbor but takes care of her bills for her and visits every week-end. She had to cut Mrs. Hale's daily spending allowance to pay down her QVC purchases."

I look up at Jared, but he's frowning down at the ground.

"She doesn't steal the cupcakes." His eyes finally meet mine, steely and cold. "I pay for them. Every day. She's not the mugger."

And with that, he turns and walks back toward the car.

I stand there for a minute, mentally berating myself. There was no way Paige or I could have known the whole story based on a few minutes of video. I knew she probably wasn't the mugger, I never even said that she was.

Jared should give me *some* brownie points for knowing something that I shouldn't. Why doesn't he?

Mixed with my large helping of chagrin is a dart of admiration. How did he see through my shtick? Any other mark would have been placated at this point.

With a sigh and one last glance at the cupcakes, I make my way slowly back toward the patrol vehicle.

He doesn't make sense to me. Why would someone pay for someone else's cupcake thievery? A cop, especially? I mean, yeah, on a purely philosophical level, I get it. The lady is old, her husband is dead, it's all very sad, but I've never seen or heard of someone doing a good deed—daily, no less—and not expecting something in return. And a cop condoning petty theft? Enabling it, even? He seems so square and severe. Why does he do it?

I don't understand him at all.

Chapter Ten

"Is the universe giving you any other hints?" Jared asks when I get back in the car with him.

"Why don't you just . . ." Stop being such an asshole? Get hit by a van, in the face? I bite my tongue. "Do whatever it is you normally do, and I'll see if anything comes to me."

He drives around, issuing speeding tickets and traffic citations, while I sit next to him and try not to breathe too much. This isn't going to work. I have nothing to contribute, and he knows it.

God, my parents were right. I am useless.

I'm ready to give up the whole thing and have him take me home. Sitting in a cop car isn't exactly my happy place as it is, and Jared's silence is grating.

But then he speaks.

"How did you know?"

"Know what?"

"About Mrs. Hale."

"I told you what I saw." The spark of vindication makes me smile. Maybe he does believe me.

"I know, but—"

We're interrupted by a burst of static from the radio.

Jared and the dispatcher toss codes and numbers back and forth. The gist seems to be kids trespassing somewhere in the woods.

"You're going to have to come with me," Jared says as we speed out of the town proper, and the scenery begins to turn into trees and mountains.

"You can't drop me off first?"

He shakes his head. "You're on the other side of town and we're the closest unit to the clearing."

"The clearing?"

"It's where the kids like to party and get in trouble. Among other things," he mutters.

I nod, but I'm not sure exactly what he's talking about.

It doesn't take very long to get to the spot. Inside of ten minutes, we pull off the main road onto a rocky dirt path that cuts through the trees. A few minutes later, the trees peter out.

His headlights reveal an open space in the middle of the woods. It's mostly gravel but there are a few grassy areas and the sky is bright with stars above us. It's pretty, even at night. No wonder people like to make out here. A handful of cars are parked in corners, all far away from each other.

When we arrive on the scene, some of the cars start up immediately and make their way out of the area, but a few stay parked and dark.

"Now what?" I say when we've sat there for a few minutes.

"Time to see what they're doing." He unbuckles his belt.

"Can I come with you?"

"Nope."

"What if one of them is the thief?"

"No one out here is stealing."

"Even criminals need a break from their wasted lives for a little love and tenderness."

"Whatever. Stay here." He gets out of the car.

I follow him.

"I told you to stay put."

"You might need me," I insist. I have to do something. Sitting in the car for the past two hours has made my ass sore. Plus I've been absolutely pathetic all night and staying put isn't going to change that.

He grumbles and stalks toward the closest car. I stay on his heels, the flashlight bobbing across the ground in front of us. The nearest vehicle is a small black compact with fogged-up windows and moans emanating from the interior.

Jared knocks on the window.

The moans and rocking continue uninterrupted.

I can't help but laugh, although I try to cover it with my hand.

Jared clears his throat, and I like to think he's muffling his own laughter, but nothing seems to crack this guy.

He knocks again, a little louder, using the butt of the flashlight to get a good rap.

This time, the moaning abruptly ceases, replaced with muffled curses.

A few long seconds pass and then the window rolls down.

"Mr. Newsome?" I say in disbelief.

Yep, it's him. The same man who got in a fight over his ex-wife at the bar the other night. And who's in the car with him? The ex-Mrs. Newsome, of course.

He doesn't have a shirt on, exposing a hairy gray chest, and his pants are unbuttoned.

"Tell them I'm not here!" Mrs. Newsome whispers loudly from the back seat.

The flashlight briefly flicks toward the back seat, and I get a foggy glimpse of Mrs. Newsome completely nude before Jared flicks the flashlight back to right above Mr. Newsome's head.

I think we both wish we could clean our retinas right about now.

"Paul," Jared says in greeting.

"Jared."

"You know you're not supposed to be out here."

"I know. We aren't causing any trouble."

"Maybe not, but you are trespassing. Have you been drinking tonight?"

"Nope, just keeping the spark alive."

Jared sighs. "Okay. Once Sheila gets dressed, why don't you two go make out somewhere that's not private property? Unless it's your own."

We leave them to their own devices, but not before they laugh loudly inside the vehicle. I can't help but laugh myself. I can't see Jared's face since he's walking in front of me, but I could swear his shoulders are shaking.

We make our way over to the other two vehicles, which are parked next to each other on the other side of the clearing.

He shines a light into the interiors of both vehicles, but they're vacant.

"What now?" I ask.

"I recognize these cars. They belong to some teenagers. They like to come out here and set bonfires and drink a bit deeper in."

"Sounds pretty normal for teenagers."

"And dangerous. Also illegal." He releases an irritated breath. "I know some spots they might be camping out at. I would ask you to return to the vehicle, but I don't think you'll listen to me."

"You are thinking correctly," I agree.

"I've got to call it in first." he says, walking back to the patrol vehicle. "It's likely we'll be driving some inebriated youngsters out of here, and if they came in two cars, they won't all fit in the back of the cruiser."

Once that's done, off into the woods we go.

"This way."

I follow him along the tree line to a deer path that leads us further into the woods. It gets darker, the branches above us blocking most of the moonlight and glow from the stars.

"Do you have an extra light?" I might not be so scared if I have something in my hands. As it is, I can only make out the shape of his back in front of me, blocking the meager beam of his flashlight.

"Nope. You could go back to the car."

"By myself, in the pitch black? You are insane."

I trudge along behind him for a few minutes. There are other paths that intersect with the one we're on, and Jared follows them confidently.

"How do you know which direction they went?"

"Because I partied out here when I was their age, too," he admits. "Some things never change."

The sound of a branch snapping in the distance makes him halt, and I crash into his back, my hands gripping his waist.

"What was that?" I ask.

"Shh."

We stand there for a few tense minutes, listening. When there are no further sounds except the far-off hoot of an owl and the faint rustling of leaves in the wind, he says, "It's probably nothing."

"Probably nothing," I say. "Except maybe a mass murderer."

"That's not likely. Branches break all the time. Or it's some kind of animal."

Silence reigns for a moment while I consider exactly what kinds of animals might be in the forest and how big their teeth might be.

"Are you going to hold onto me all night?"

I quickly let go, not realizing I was still grasping his waist.

"Sorry," I mutter.

We resume our walk again down the darkened path.

After a few more minutes, I hear laughter and voices.

"Do you hear that?" I whisper.

"Yes," Jared answers, a bit tersely. We keep walking in the direction of the voices.

"I think that's their fire." I'm still whispering.

"I know."

The illumination is to our right, a bit off the beaten path in the middle of what looks like a copse of trees.

We stop walking and he shines his light up a little in the direction of their fire. We can walk through the thick of it toward them, but a slew of branches and dead leaves are in the way and the ground is uneven.

"We probably won't be able to get through there without making a lot of noise and alerting them to our presence," I say.

"I *know*,"

I can't quite make out the conversation, but they seem to be having a grand time, whatever they're doing. There are probably eight to ten of them, ranging in age from sixteen to eighteen. Someone yells something and then music kicks on, a loud punk song.

"The music should mask our steps," I say.

"Stay here." He steps off the path, over a tree stump, and toward the party.

"What? No way." I follow behind him.

"You're going to hurt yourself."

"I am not."

He turns around to face me, shining the light down between us. "This ground is uneven and you don't have a flashlight."

"So give me yours."

"That's not happening."

"I'm not standing out here waiting for some creature to eat me."

"There are no creatures out here."

"You just said there's wild animals."

Even though I can't make out his expression clearly, I can sense his eye roll.

He doesn't bother responding. He turns around and keeps walking.

"I'll be fine if you don't get so far ahead of me," I say, hurrying to catch up. As long as I stay close to him, I can follow his steps.

Except, as I'm hurrying toward him, I trip over a rock or something and launch straight toward his back. He turns at the last minute and tries to catch me before I fall. We both tumble to the hard earth, him on his back and me on top of him.

I can't breathe for a moment, the wind nearly knocked out

of me. I lie there clutching at him, his badge digging into my right palm. The flashlight is lying a few feet away, its feeble light shining in our direction, exposing Jared's face in varying degrees of brightness and shadow.

"I'm sorry," I say as soon as my breath returns. The faint brush of his cologne against my senses makes me breathe in deeply.

I brace myself, ready to face his wrath, sure that he'll point out how he told me to stay in the car and to stay on the trail and by not listening I brought all of this on myself and him. And he would be completely correct.

Instead, his hands clutch my arms and his eyes search my face. "Are you okay?"

I'm struck speechless.

Should I say yes? If I say yes, and he's assured of my relative safety, will I then have to face his contempt?

"I think so." I choose wisely. "Are you okay?" He landed on his back and there's so much rubble on the forest floor, it's possible he's injured. I had a cushioned landing, although the hard chest beneath my hands is anything but soft.

"Yeah," he answers in a whisper.

I don't move. I can't move. I realize suddenly that I'm straddling him. He must realize it at the same time because his eyes widen and his breathing falters.

An image flits through my brain. Me, on top of him, sans clothes. I suck in a breath, and heat rushes to my core. I have the sudden urge to grind my center against his to see if what's between his legs is as hard as the rest of him. But I don't.

He shuts his eyes tightly for a second, his hands tightening around my arms, and then he's shifting beneath me, encouraging me to get up and move away so he can grab his flashlight and stand. His hands reach for me again when I wobble over a stray branch, but then he seems to realize what he's doing. His hand drops to his side and he asks again, "You okay?"

"Fine." But my heart is beating wildly and my palms are sweating and I'm definitely not fine.

Jared is staring at me, and his gaze is like the fire of a thousand suns. Or something slightly less dramatic.

I take a breath. "Let's go get these kids. I'll stay out of the way while you do your thing," I promise, my tone clipped and professional.

"Right." He turns and I follow him toward the noise.

Chapter Eleven

H E KNOWS the teens partying in the woods, of course. A town this small, I wouldn't be surprised if he could recite all of their Social Security numbers from memory.

I listen and watch while he orders some of them to put out the fire and another few to help pick up the beer bottles and trash. Then he talks to each of them and tells them what's going to happen next.

Then we march out of the woods.

Luckily, they brought lanterns and flashlights. It's not hard to follow the group through the trees and back to where the cars are parked. The kids are mostly subdued, if a bit giggly despite the circumstances.

By the time we reach the clearing, a couple more patrol cars have arrived.

I stand by Jared's car, leaning my butt against the hood, and watch while the kids are issued citations and then divvyed up among the drivers.

Troy is one of them. He walks over to greet me, the head-lights of one of the cars illuminating his legs as he walks.

"Hey, Troy."

"How's it going so far?"

"Pretty exciting, but no real leads." I shrug. "It's been . . ." I glance over at Jared, who's coordinating who gets in which car. "Interesting."

Jared comes back over before we can chat any further about my epic fail of a night. "You're taking the kids who live in the heights," he tells Troy. "I'll take these kids." He motions to the ones standing behind him. "Anderson has the rest."

"Will do, boss. See you around, Ruby." Troy tosses me a grin before striding off to take his assigned kids to their respective homes.

We get in the car and it's a silent ride to drop off the kids. At each house, Jared gets out and talks to the parents before coming back to the car.

Then he takes me home.

I feel the need to save face before I leave him for the night.

"I'm sorry tonight was pretty much a bust. I was worried this would happen. It's why I was reluctant to . . . offer my services."

I watch his profile in the light of the dash. He glances over at me once, briefly, but his eyes are as dark and unreadable as ever.

"I'm sorry, too," he says, surprising me. "I shouldn't have been so hard on you about the cupcakes. It's just . . . I really think the whole psychic thing is bullshit."

"Really? I couldn't tell."

His lips twitch and then he shrugs. "I don't want people I care about to get hurt."

He pulls up in front of the house.

"I'm not going to hurt anyone." Before he can say anything else, I get out with a hurried goodbye.

He waits until I'm inside before pulling away.

In the living room, Paige and Tabby are passed out on the couch. There's popcorn and cookies strewn all over the dining table and the TV is still on. They both have freshly painted nails and Tabby has a smudge of chocolate on her cheek.

I shut off the TV and make sure both of them are covered up with blankets. Before heading up to bed myself, I stop and watch them sleeping peacefully.

I'm not going to hurt anyone.

I don't know if I spoke the truth.

～

"Do you need a pencil?"

"I'm fine."

"What about paper?"

"No, Charlotte, it's fine."

"Can I kiss you goodbye in front of your new friends?"

"Charlotte!"

Two mornings later, Paige is starting school.

I walk with her to the campus and we get her registered. The elderly woman in the office is a volunteer and half blind and any worries I had about getting Paige registered without some kind of legal guardianship documents is put to rest when she thinks I'm Paige's mom anyway and doesn't even ask for ID for me or a birth certificate for Paige.

Once she has her class list, Paige ditches me without a second glance.

"Make good choices. No conning classmates, but don't be anyone's patsy," I call after her as she practically runs away from me.

Teenagers.

Yesterday, I even took her to the only store in town that sells clothes for people under sixty and bought her two new outfits, and this is the treatment I get.

I walk back home alone, make coffee, and sit on the porch. Mr. Bingel is out trimming his roses, so I have a pretty good time listening to him grumble.

It sounds like he's reminiscing about how wonderful his life was before we moved in next door and how I never take the time to clip my own roses and his house would look so much better if "that girl" took care of her yard.

"Will you show me how to take care of my roses?" I ask loudly enough that he can hear.

Mr. Bingel studiously ignores me and continues with his snipping and muttering.

Jared runs by.

It must be eight thirty. He seems to run by every morning around the same time.

I wave, but he doesn't even peep over at the house.

Sigh.

Gravy the devil cat is also outside. He's found a sunny spot at my feet, perfect for cleaning his nether regions.

When he stops and lies still, I try to pet him and he hisses.

Everyone in this town loves me.

I finish my coffee around the same time Mr. Bingel finishes clipping his bushes. I don't know how he maintains such a meticulous yard, and he's never dirty. His gloves and shoes are always pristine, despite kneeling on the ground. It's like even the dirt is afraid to offend him. Although, when he stands, he seems to be favoring his right hip. Maybe his bones are deteriorating from the force of his disapproval.

I know he's lonely. No one ever comes over to see him, and he spends more time on his garden than anything else. Secretly, I think he likes us living next to him. Why else would he be coming outside, trimming his already perfectly groomed roses?

"You okay there, Mr. Bingel?"

He still ignores me, gathering his things and shuffling inside. I'm about to leave, too, since my task for the morning—bother Mr. Bingel into being my friend—has failed miserably, but before I stand up, a patrol car stops in front of my house.

Troy exits the vehicle and lopes up to the house with what I've come to recognize as his usual cocky swagger. He has a manila file folder in his hand.

"Hey, Ruby." He takes a seat on the porch swing next to me.

"What's up?"

"Don't you already know?"

I sigh. "You brought me the case files from the mugging?"

"How did you know that?" His voice is filled with exaggerated incredulity. "Wait, don't tell me. The spirits told you."

"I'm not a medium, Troy," I say with a smile. "The file is right there and it has Cassie's name on it."

His smile drops into an openmouthed stare. "You *are* psychic."

"It's a real gift."

We laugh and he nudges me with his shoulder good-naturedly.

"So Jared said it didn't go real well the other night," he says.

"Yeah. I thought I had a lead, but it didn't have anything to do with the mugging."

"That's okay." He slaps my knee. "It's still pretty weird that you knew about Jared buying those cupcakes for Mrs. Hale every day. He never tells anyone about that stuff. Anyway," he puts the folder on my lap, "I thought maybe this might help you, you know, sense stuff or whatever."

"Thanks."

I should have thought to ask for the file myself. I really know nothing more than that Cassie was mugged outside the restaurant and a bag was put over her head.

I open the folder and glance at the contents. There's a statement signed by Cassie with a list of what was in her purse, a picture of the bag used during the mugging, and photos of the crime scene.

"Where's this bag from?" I pick up the photo and peer at it. It's a large canvas bag with lettering on it.

He gets closer, peering over my shoulder. "It's from this old Greek restaurant that closed down a few years ago. Jared already checked into it when we couldn't get any usable prints from the bag—fabric is too porous. Apparently, when the restaurant shut down, all of their bags were auctioned to the same buyer. They don't know who it was because it was done through a resale agency."

"Which resale agency?"

"Jared's looking into that. It's his job to find out all those hard-hitting details."

"What's your job?"

"To look pretty."

I laugh.

"Come on, Ruby. You can't deny it. I make this look good." He nods his head slowly and purses his lips.

"You're right, I can't deny it."

"So listen, Tabby wanted me to invite you and Paige over for dinner tomorrow night at her place. It's a weekly thing we do. There will be a few close friends and she thought you might like to meet some more people. I'll be there, and so will Jared, Ben, and you'll get to meet Mrs. Olsen. A good time will be had by all." He nods sagely, and for some reason, I don't believe him.

"I'm not sure," I hedge. "We're really busy right now. Paige just started school today and the grand opening is in a week."

And I still have to get upstairs to the office and look over video files for information. Hopefully something better than those damn cupcakes.

"You realize if you say no to me now, Tabby will be all over you like red on a fire truck. She will drag you kicking and screaming if she has to. She doesn't like hearing the word 'no' about anything. And don't tell her I told you this, but you've probably figured it out for yourself. She doesn't have many friends, at least not in the same age range."

My resolve wavers. Paige will probably want to go, too. And I've never been good at telling her no.

I nod. "We'll go."

"Awesome." He slaps me on the knee again as he stands, leaving the file with me. "Dinner starts at six." He turns and points at me. "I'll pick you guys up." He doesn't give me a chance to argue, waving goodbye and jogging back to the patrol car.

Chapter Twelve

"How was school? Everything you ever dreamed?"

Paige rolls her eyes. "It was school. There were teachers and kids and learning. And that's it." She stalks past me toward the stairs. I've been lying in wait in the front office, unloading one of Ruby's shipments. This one has crystals and herbs and an assortment of clothing from wavy scarves to tie-dyed shirts.

Paige stops before leaving the room and smiles at me. "I made a friend."

Then she runs off.

"It better not be a boy!" I call after her.

As soon as she disappears up the stairs and no one is watching, I do a happy dance. She likes school! Well, she doesn't hate it, at least. If she did, she would have let me know right away. And a friend! Even though we have to leave in a few months, before Ruby gets back, at least she'll have some kind of normal memory to take with her and hopefully the ability to make even more friends in the future. The thought of leaving, starting over somewhere else, makes the happy dance falter. I wanted consistency and normalcy for Paige, not running away, not having to move. Again.

I have to talk to her about the dinner at Tabby's, and about what I found on the videotapes while she was at school, but I'll have to wait.

I know Paige well enough that she'll need a few minutes to decompress. She's always been a pretty social child, but she wears out easily when she's around a lot of people for extended periods. Especially new people.

I put a frozen lasagna in the oven and start on a salad, waiting for her to emerge from the bedroom. I got a small paycheck from the police department, but it was only enough to buy some supplies for the grand opening and cover us for food for the week. Mostly premade, frozen, or microwavable food. But food is food.

She finally comes down to the kitchen, no longer in her new clothes but dressed down in her ratty flannel PJ pants, hair up in a messy ponytail.

"Tell me about your friend."

"Her name is Naomi. She lives a couple of blocks away. Can I sleep over at her house?"

A sleepover! It's like we're real people. I force my features to remain calm. "When it's not a school night and I can meet her parents."

She grins and leans a hip against the counter, watching me chop tomatoes.

"I'm glad you had a good day."

"What about you?" she asks.

"We're invited to dinner at Tabby's tomorrow night. Oh,

and I found something of interest on the videos that we might be able to use."

Her eyes light up. "You did?"

"I'll show you after dinner. And after you get your homework done."

She groans. "Cruel sister."

"Yep."

She eats in record time, chatting about the kids at school—there aren't many of them—and the teachers—they're all nice—and Naomi—who's a year older than her and oh so cool.

Homework is only a few pages of math, which she flies through without needing assistance. Thank god, because I don't know anything about math. I went to so many different schools growing up and wasn't enrolled consistently. I barely scraped through my GED when I was sixteen.

When she's done, we head upstairs to the office.

"Here." I hand her the file that Troy brought me. "Check out the picture of the bag used in the mugging."

She peers at it while I warm up the computer.

"Check this out." I turn the screen toward her and show her the video footage I found at the restaurant. It's another elderly woman, but this time instead of disappearing cupcakes, she's piling some leftovers into a canvas bag.

"It's the same type of bag."

"Troy said the bags are from an old Greek restaurant that's not around anymore. And they sold all the bags to the same person before they left town."

"Another old lady." Paige gives me a look. "We better make sure this intel is good. What if she bought them from someone else or something?"

"Which is why we need to get more information, and I know how we're going to do that."

"How?"

"See this?" I point at the paused image on the screen. The woman is wearing a button-up vest covered in giant green cats.

Paige nods.

"Tabby told me about someone in town who only wears cat-covered clothes. Mrs. Olsen."

"The same lady she calls her grandma?"

"Yep. And guess who's going to be at Tabby's dinner party this weekend?"

"Mrs. Olsen."

"Right."

"So how exactly are we going to find out if she's the mugger?"

"*We're* not." I give her a pointed look. "*I'm* going to track down these bags. I just have to get her alone," I say with a grin.

The next day, Troy picks up Paige and me, and we arrive at Tabby's right after six o'clock. The first thing I notice is Jared standing in the corner, talking to a blond woman. Her back is to me, and I don't think I've seen her before.

It's not remarkable to me that he's talking to a woman, but he's smiling.

It's not a large smile. Most might not even notice it, but there's a definite curving of his lips and tilting of his eyes. If it was just the lips, I might excuse it as a false smile, but the eyes never lie.

For some reason, it bothers me.

I've never seen him smile like that.

Maybe because when he's around me, he mostly frowns.

The second thing I notice is Tabby talking to Ben the bartender, and she's also smiling, but there's tension around her eyes.

Fighting again, I suppose.

In total, there are about half a dozen people gathered in her living room having pre-dinner drinks. Jared, the mystery woman, Tabby, Ben, an elderly lady who must be Mrs. Olsen because she's wearing a sweater with a giant orange cat on the front, and another older woman in a wheelchair with her head back, mouth open, eyes shut. She's either sleeping or dead. I hope she's sleeping. I can't tell if she's breathing.

Everyone is dressed casually, and I'm glad because I don't own much more than the worn jeans and faded T-shirt I'm currently wearing.

When Tabby sees us, she comes over and gives both Paige and I hugs before introducing us to the people we don't know.

The mystery blond is Eleanor Rogers. She's the town librarian. Eleanor looks like her name sounds, regal with a thin face and a thinner nose. She's pale and her eyes are serious behind her wire-rimmed glasses.

Mrs. Olsen is the sweater-cat lady and also definitely the woman from the video. Paige immediately sits next to her and starts asking her about where she got her sweater.

The sleeper is Miss Viola. Tabby can't make introductions since the woman is apparently passed out. "Too many Moscow Mules," Tabby tells me.

"Introductions are done, let's go get a drink," Troy says, leading me in the direction of the kitchen.

Tabby follows us there. "Ben is such a bag of dicks," she says once the door to the living room swings shut.

"Then why did you invite him?" I ask.

She pulls a bottle of beer out of the fridge, opens it, and hands it to me. "Because he's Troy's best friend." She waves a hand toward her brother. "We have dinner every week, ever since we were kids."

"Don't blame me," Troy says, hands up. "You could have totally uninvited us both and I wouldn't have complained."

"Don't be an ass. You know we never miss weekly dinner."

"You could not invite Ben," Troy insists. "I wouldn't care."

"I have to."

"Why? You guys drive each other crazy."

"I know. I should just fuck him and get it over with."

Troy chokes on his drink and coughs a few times. "Dude," he says with a grimace, "I don't want to hear that."

"What?" She makes a belligerent face at him and takes a swig of her own beer. "Come on, Ruby."

She grabs my arm and leans in to whisper into my ear as we walk toward the living room. "Mrs. Olsen invited Eleanor. She's been trying to hook Jared up with her all year. I thought she had given up, but then she called me today and told me Eleanor was coming. You'll have to tell me what you think later. Any visions of wedding bells when you touch her." She laughs and waggles her eyebrows at me.

I take a long drink of the beer in my hand.

After a few minutes of chitchat in the living room, the timer on the stove dings, and Tabby calls us into the dining room for dinner.

Mrs. Olsen maneuvers Miss Viola to the table, and then

everyone gets situated in their seats. I end up sandwiched between Mrs. Olson and Jared.

There's a spaghetti casserole that Mrs. Olson made—I know this because she tells me three times between sitting down and passing the dishes around the table—along with a fancy salad that Tabby prepared and garlic bread that Jared brought.

The conversation flows around me as I dish food onto my plate.

"Tabby says you're psychic," Mrs. Olsen says to me.

"Ruby's helping Jared and Troy catch the Castle Cove Bandit," Tabby says.

"How are you helping?" Mrs. Olsen asks.

"Well, it's a bit complicated."

"Can you tell the future?"

"I give people readings. I can't always see specifics, but if people have questions they're trying to answer, or need guidance in some way, I might be able to help."

"I have questions. Like why are all these people still single?" She gestures around the room and then looks over at me with a gleam in her eye. "I hear you're single, too."

"Um." I shoot Tabby a dirty look. "Yes," then carefully add, "but I'm not looking for anything right now."

Mrs. Olsen harrumphs. "Well. That's a shame. We've run outta females of appropriate age, and this big lug over here"— she points at Troy with her fork—"needs a woman."

He pauses, his food halfway to his mouth. "What the hell, Grandma?"

She keeps talking. "It's been forever since we've had a wedding here in town. Kids these days either leave or stay here and stay single. It's terrible." Her eyes focus like a laser in Jared's direction. "Like this one here." She motions to him with her fork. "There's only a few single women who are nice and have decent jobs, like Eleanor over there." Eyes swing in that direction.

I feel bad for Eleanor for a moment, she squirms so much under the attention, but Mrs. Olsen doesn't seem to notice or care. Or both.

I take a long drink of my beer and hope the attention stays off of me.

"But what do they do about it? Nothing." She harrumphs again. "And don't get me started on Tabby." I smother a laugh.

"Grandma," Tabby says calmly, "I will stab you with my fork." She holds it up as proof.

The words roll right by Mrs. Olsen. "There's a fine young man working in her shop. What's his name? Peter?"

"Jack," Tabby says through clenched teeth. "And it's not happening."

I can't help but glance over at Ben. He doesn't show any reaction other than his hand clenching slightly around his fork.

"You young people don't even date anymore, it's terrible. Your generation does nothing but Chatbook and Twatter and Snapface."

"None of that is accurate," Tabby says.

Mrs. Olsen continues as if Tabby hasn't spoken at all. "Everything is done on the computer. There's no human inter-action. No wonder there are no weddings or babies."

"Babies?" I mouth toward Tabby, but she rolls her eyes.

Everyone is silent for a few moments after that pronounce-ment, eating and studiously avoiding eye contact. No one wants to get Mrs. Olsen talking again.

Then Troy, brave soul that he is, clears his throat. "So is everyone going to the festival next weekend?"

And with that, there's a burst of chatter, everyone grateful for the subject change.

When dinner ends, Mrs. Olsen mentions wanting to bring leftovers to the nursing home.

Paige and I insist on helping her pack up since we were the only ones who didn't provide any dishes. Thankfully there isn't too much flack or offers of help from everyone else.

We're in the kitchen—Mrs. Olsen, Paige, and myself—when I set the plan into action and steer the conversation where we need it to go.

"Does Tabby have any of those canvas bags?" I ask Mrs. Olsen. "You know, like the big, thick ones. That would be perfect for carrying these leftovers out of here."

She doesn't take the bait though. She shrugs and heads toward the living room. "I can ask her."

"Wait," Paige says. "I think I saw some in the front hall. They were blue and white with weird letters on them."

"Okay, I'll go look there," Mrs. Olsen says, turning to leave again.

"Wait." Now it's my turn. Mrs. Olsen is not making this very easy. "I think I saw you the other day in the store, and you had a bag just like it. Do you still have it? That would be perfect. It looked really big and roomy."

"Oh yeah, I got that bag from the old Greek restaurant when they closed. They had a huge sale, I got eighty percent off. I bought ten of those bags."

I exchange a look with Paige.

"It was a real shame when they all got stolen," she adds.

"Stolen? All of them?"

"Yep. Well, all but one. It was about three weeks ago. I took Miss Viola to the boardwalk and had them in her lap because they ran out of those little carts. Pushing Miss Viola around is like having an extra cart anyway. I turned around for one second and that's all it took. Poof. Gone."

Paige and I make eye contact. She shrugs, and I know we're both thinking the same thing. We didn't have any cameras set up three weeks ago that could have caught the perp. Anyone could have taken those bags. They're long gone at this point, unless we catch someone on camera using them besides Mrs. Olsen.

What am I supposed to tell Jared the next time he asks?

Chapter Thirteen

I SPEND the next few days watching video footage of Castle Cove instead of what I should be doing, which is readying the shop for the grand opening this weekend.

I still need to fix the display case that Gravy broke, but I haven't the first idea how to do it. It's too big, I'll probably need to find the money to purchase an entirely new display, but . . . I don't even have a dry bed to sleep in at this point.

There's nothing useful on the videos, no more canvas bags. I do see Tabby making out with Ben, which I promptly turn off and delete, guilt niggling at me for even the little glimpse I got. And I see Jared paying for Mrs. Hale's cupcakes, which also makes me feel guilty. Damn him.

I do tip him off about Mrs. Olsen being the purchaser of the canvas bags, even though I know it's a dead end. At least I have something to offer by using my "abilities."

We need better intel though, and soon.

When Paige gets home, we eat dinner, she does her homework, and then she takes a turn at watching the surveillance footage while I work on unloading the shipments that have come in.

"Houston, we have a problem," Paige says, coming into the front shop.

"What's up?"

"One of the cameras slipped. The gas station."

I put down the box of unicorn figurines that I'd been unwrapping and face her. "They're still open. You run distraction and I'll fix it."

She nods.

The wire attachment to the small video piece is faulty. Luckily, I brought a few things with me to fix any potential issues. I use a bread tie to quickly re-attach the small lens while Paige buys a pack of gum at the counter, and then we're done.

When we get to our street, there's a truck idling at the curb.

Tabby is at the tailgate. "Hey," she calls out when we get closer. "I brought you something."

We round the truck to see what she's doing. Ben's with her; the truck must be his. They're hauling a large wooden object out of the back of the truck.

"Is that . . . ?" Paige asks.

"I built you a new shelf!" Tabby says, clapping her hands.

"You made this?" I'm stunned. It looks nicer than the one Gravy broke. Dark wood that matches the rest of the shelving, but with bright new glass, and the corners are carved with an elaborate wood trim.

She shrugs. "It's no biggie. Help us carry it inside."

Paige runs to open the door while Ben, Tabby, and I haul it up the porch steps and inside.

"I can never pay you back for this," I say, still in shock after we set it where the old unit was.

"You don't have to."

"Why would you do this for me?"

She's baffled. "Why wouldn't I do this for you?"

Because I'm a fraud. "You barely know me."

"Yeah, but you're a good egg." She pats me on the arm.

If only you knew.

"You can repay me by working our booth at the Bike, Fish, and Cookie Festival."

"The what?" Paige and I ask in unison.

Ben pipes up. "It starts tomorrow. It's normally later in the month, but they're demolishing the old sock building on the boardwalk and they didn't want all the debris to block the foot traffic."

"Bike, Fish, and Cookie Festival?" My brows lift. "That's . . . weird."

Tabby nods. "Yeah, we have a different festival like every month. There used to be more than one a month and it was getting way out of hand, so they started combining them. They tried to keep similar items together, like the Lobster and Eel Festival, but at the end there was a bunch of random things we have to celebrate so they just threw them together."

"Okay," I say, because what else can I say?

"Since your grand opening is Saturday, I figured you could help me at the booth on Friday and we can pass out more flyers to help you get some business, too." She beams.

I don't deserve her friendship. I still can't quite wrap my head around why she's so nice to me. I guess it makes sense if what Troy said is true, that she's a bit lonely for company and I am the only other woman around under forty—other than Eleanor. But still. She doesn't have to do all these things.

"That's awesome!" Paige says.

"That's great." My voice isn't as excited as it should be. I'm a bit blindsided, actually.

Ben and Tabby leave. Paige rambles on about school and Naomi and some project they're working on about osmosis. I go through the motions, nodding and smiling when I should, but inside I'm brimming with guilt.

They're helping Ruby, not me. If they only knew . . . Paige laughs at something and I try to snap out of it, if only for her sake.

"I can't wait until Friday." She grins at me.

"Me either."

It's not totally a lie.

I can't sleep, so I keep an eye on the videos. The only store that's open this late is the gas station, and the damn camera slips again.

"Ugh," I tell it.

It's pointed at an angle toward the floor, so now I can only see people's shoes as they walk by and part of the ground next to one of the coolers in the back. Not helpful at all.

I play around on the internet, keeping an eye on the cameras in my periphery.

The gas station closes at ten on weeknights. The video goes dark and gray, along with the rest of the cameras. It's hopeless. But for some reason, I stay in the office, googling things like, *why does my hair suck* and *how to get over being raised by terrible people* while watching the darkened screens. I'm contemplating where I went wrong with my life when I see motion.

"Someone's at the gas station," I say to the empty room.

I can still only see the ground, but something is definitely happening. Something not right at all. There are things smashing on the ground. Pieces flying everywhere, the spray of liquid. A droplet even hits the small lens, making everything blurry.

Heart racing, I pick up the phone and dial.

The activity causes the small camera to slip even further, and all I can see is the bottom corner of the shelf, but I keep watching.

Whoever is in there must run to leave because their shoelace gets caught on the corner of the shelf—the only shelf I can see. It must be a cheap shoe because the lace rips, leaving a frayed strand behind.

A few minutes later, there's a knock at the door.

I check on Paige, who's still fast asleep, before running to the door.

It's Jared, and he looks grim. "There's been a break-in."

"I know. I called it in."

"I know." His lips purse slightly and then he turns to walk to his patrol car idling at the curb. "Are you coming?" he calls when he's halfway to his car and I'm still standing at the door.

His words jerk me into motion. I lock the front door and follow him.

"Troy's securing the scene," he says when we're driving down the road. "Someone did some damage."

I nod. It should only take us a minute to get there, maybe less.

"How did you know?"

I shrug. "Same as always. Just sensed something being off there."

I can feel the weight of his eyes on me but keep my face turned forward.

Only Troy and one other cop are there when we arrive—Anderson, according to Jared. He barks orders immediately.

This isn't a crime scene like on TV. There's no CSI, no lab coats; just Jared, Troy, Anderson, and a sleepy owner who must have been called in.

"Boss," Troy calls from the front of the store, holding up a bag half full of food.

It's the same type of canvas bag that was used in Cassie's mugging.

I listen to them talk and move myself over to the hidden camera. I need to get it out of here before they find it and where it's streaming to.

There's some money missing from the register, and it looks like the perp took some food, too. Some of the displays have been ravaged, littering chips and candy on the floor.

The main destruction is at the back, part of which my camera captured.

The perp opened up the back fridge where the beer was stored and broke a crap ton of bottles on the ground. It reeks of stale beer.

I survey the damage while hiding the small device at my back so I can surreptitiously shove it into the pocket of my sweater when no one is looking.

I bend down, like I'm examining the floor, and pick up the frayed piece of shoelace as well, hiding it along with the camera. It might come in handy later when I need information to share.

"Someone wasted a lot of beer," Troy says, shaking his head. "Damn shame."

"They were angry," I say.

Eyes swing toward me.

"What makes you say that?" the cop named Anderson asks. He's older than Troy and Jared, maybe midforties. Gray around the temples, thin, with a slight beer belly.

I look around at the broken glass spread around the floor. "It takes a lot of rage to slam this many bottles to the ground hard enough to break most of them."

Only a few bottles slid around and escaped unscathed.

Jared's gaze focuses on the owner, a portly man with a receding hairline. "Anyone angry at you, Billy?"

"Not that I know of."

"Anyone strange loitering around lately?"

"Nope."

Jared sighs and scrubs a hand through his hair. "Great. Half the town shops here, so prints won't be real useful. Again. Troy, bag the items you have. They should lift easier from there than from the bag." His gaze lasers on me. "Any other feelings you want to share? Maybe something including a description of our suspect?"

I shake my head. "No."

We don't stay long. I wait around while Troy and Anderson bag up items to be sent out for prints.

Jared talks to the owner to get information on what happened up until closing. Nothing unusual; he locked up at ten and went home, then got the call about thirty minutes later.

When they're all done, Jared drives me home.

It's a silent ride.

I should be happier. I finally, actually contributed to the investigation. Sort of. They still don't have any leads, but at least I have something more concrete to help convince Jared I'm not a fraud.

Then why do I feel so terrible?

"I'm sorry I couldn't help more," I offer when the silence starts to get to me.

"No, you don't need to apologize. Thanks for calling it in. It's not your fault, and I . . ." He clears his throat and pulls over in front of the house, puts the car in park, and turns to face me. "I should be the one apologizing."

Well now he's done it. He's struck me speechless.

"I haven't been fair to you," he says. "I have no excuse other than being obnoxiously protective of the people who live here, but you've done nothing to deserve the way I've been treating you."

If only he knew.

I wonder if familiarity has bred affection. It's a common ploy that my parents use to a certain extent, with long cons especially. But even with quick ones, it can be effective. If a mark sees the same person at a coffee shop every morning, even just for a few days, eventually they become somewhat familiar. That person can then approach the mark, and simple recognition will make the mark more trusting.

Inadvertently using one of my parents' tricks makes my stomach churn.

"It's fine, you're forgiven." I try to smile, but the motion feels clumsy and my face is inexplicably flushed and I'm more uncomfortable in his presence now than I was when he was being straight-up rude.

I open the door to leave.

"Wait." He reaches out, putting his hand over mine.

I stare at his hand, swallow, and then meet his eyes.

I'm used to seeing Jared frowning at me with dark eyes and

an icy expression. What I'm not used to is apologetic, warm eyes and a slight smile.

"Let me give you my number," he says, his hand still on mine. "That way if you have anything else to share, you can call me directly and don't have to go through dispatch."

I nod.

He pulls out a small notepad and writes his number on it before handing me the paper.

I take it and race into the house without saying good night.

I stare down at his number. There's no way I'm calling him.

$$Chapter\ Fourteen$$

THE BIKE, Fish, and Cookie Festival starts on Thursday and lasts through the weekend. It's being held at the fairgrounds, which are located just north of the boardwalk—a broad expanse of space that's been filled with booths and a Ferris wheel.

"How does the hardware store fit in with this festival?" I ask when I arrive early Friday morning to set up the booth, a tray of cookies in hand and a stack of flyers in my purse.

Tabby begged me to bake cookies, even brought over the ingredients, thankfully, since my cupboards are woefully bare.

"We have some fishing gear and some replacement bike parts at the shop. And now, cookies. Bike, fish, cookies." She ticks each item off on her fingers.

I put the tray on a table and she immediately sneaks her hand under the plastic wrapping and grabs one.

She takes a bite and makes a face. "Is this oatmeal?"

"I made chocolate chip, too."

She puts the half-eaten oatmeal cookie back on the tray and

inspects the cookies closely before picking out a chocolate chip one instead.

"What exactly do you want me to do here?" I ask.

Everything has already been set up. Various items are displayed on shelves and cases in the booth, and I brought the cookies that she's currently eating.

"You're going to help me attract customers to the booth. And pass out your flyers. I can put some over here by the register, too."

"How am I going to attract customers?"

"Come on." She stuffs the rest of the cookie in her mouth and jumps off the table, wiping her hands on her pants. "I got something for you," she says around her mouthful of food.

She takes me around to the back of the booth where there's a flap in the tent and a small private area. She points out some additional supplies, a cooler with waters and sandwiches, and some clothes hanging on a portable clothes rack.

"Here." She pulls an item wrapped in plastic off the rack and hands it to me.

"What is this?"

"Your uniform." She grins. "Get dressed and come out when you're ready. You should probably take off your pants and shirt. It gets hot in there."

She disappears back into the front, dropping the tent flap behind her so I'm left alone.

I sit on a metal folding chair and unwrap the item in my hands.

"Tabby." I stick my head out of the tent flap after putting on the outfit she gave me. "I'm not wearing this."

"You have to."

"I do not."

"You promised to help me."

"I promised to help, not wear . . . whatever this is."

She laughs.

"What, exactly, is this?"

"It's our Bike, Fish, and Cookie Festival costume."

"I look like a mermaid on crack."

"Oh, come on, let me see. It's not that bad."

After a quick glance around—only a few people are milling about since it's still early—I step out from behind the curtain so she can see the whole outfit. I have to hold the back in place because there's some kind of tie that I couldn't reach while stepping into the monstrosity.

At the top of the costume is a foam cookie that surrounds my head, with a big hole for me to put my face through. The body is a black bicycle, one tire over my top and one over my bottom, and then there's a fish tail that doesn't quite cover my legs. I have to hold the fin up in one hand. The whole thing looks like it was sewn together by a blind person with two left hands. Which means Tabby probably made it.

"Dude." There's a gleam in her eyes that I don't like the look of. "Yes!"

"Dude. No," I say.

"You look hot."

"Are you insane?"

She tilts her head. "Most of the time."

"Can I take this off now?"

"Hell no, this is like a rite of passage. Do you need me to tie it in the back?"

"I don't need you to do anything," I grumble. I'd much rather take it off, but I suppose a promise is a promise. She did build me that shelving unit and babysit Paige for free, and she's been nothing but nice to me. I don't understand why anyone would be nice and not want something in return. Although now that I'm wearing this costume from hell, I'm beginning to understand her motives a bit more.

I turn around and let her tie me up, against my better judgment.

"So, why exactly do I have to dress like this?"

She tugs on the costume behind me, making it tighter around my waist. "You're the lure."

"Why can't you be the lure?"

"I was the lure yesterday. We need fresh meat to draw in the sharks."

"Sharks?"

"You know, customers." She finishes tying me up and I turn around.

"What do I do now?"

"I wrote a song for you to sing."

My mouth drops open. "Are you kidding me?"

"Yeah." She laughs. "You should have seen your face. There's no song." Then her eyes light up. "But maybe we can write one."

She's kidding. I think. "Why would you need a song, anyway?"

"Sales have been terrible." She straightens out some items on a shelf. "Mr. Collins across the way keeps stealing the customers with his fancy cheese."

I glance over to see Mr. Collins grinning at us. He's an old guy in a wheelchair with a floppy hat and sunglasses. His booth has items similar to Tabby's.

"That's cheating, Mr. Collins," Tabby yells. "This isn't the cheese festival."

He waves at us, still grinning.

"I hates him," Tabby grumbles.

"We can beat him at this game."

"We can?" Her brows lift.

"Of course."

It's easy. As soon as there are people wandering in our direction, I use some tried and true carnie tricks. I hide most of the cookies down on one of the shelves, out of sight, and then call out to people as they pass. "Only two cookies left over here! We've barely opened and they're disappearing quick! Get 'em while you can before they run out!"

That's all it takes. The outfit probably does help. It's one of those things you can't look away from. Once people think they might be missing out on something, they're quick to head over. And once there are a few, it naturally draws in more. When people see a crowd forming, they want to know what's going on.

Once Tabby's booth gets busy, we stay distracted all morning. Most of the people I don't recognize, likely from neighboring towns and counties who came up for the day for the festival.

I still feel ridiculous in the costume, but something warm blooms in my chest when I see how happy Tabby is to have one-upped Mr. Collins. It's almost enough to get rid of the embarrassment. Almost.

The embarrassment intensifies when Troy and Jared show up in their uniforms, all put together and official.

I look like a weirdo.

Troy grins at me. "You wear the costume of death well."

"Costume of death?" I keep my gaze focused on Troy. I

cannot bring myself to face Jared's reaction to this absurd getup.

"I had to wear it one year when we were having a warmer than usual spring and I thought I was gonna die." He peers at the costume with a grimace. "I sweated in this thing like a pig. I doubt Tabby's washed it since."

Ugh. Gross. I make a face.

"I get out of it every year by volunteering for overtime."

Jared laughs.

And now I'm forced to look at him. Have I ever heard him laugh before? The sound is as startling as it is attractive. His head goes back, exposing white teeth and a strong throat. I swallow and try to focus on the conversation. "Good to know," I say. "I'll keep that in mind for next year."

He's smiling at me, and there's no trace of disgust in his expression. I suppose I have that going for me.

"How long have you guys had this . . . costume?" I ask Troy.

"Since they started the Bike, Fish, and Cookie Festival years ago." He smiles and his eyes soften a little bit. "My mom made it."

The ludicrousness of being in the costume melts a little bit at his words. This is obviously a family tradition, and even though it's weird, it's nice to be included in something. I wonder if someday Paige and I will have some family traditions other than swindling people.

"Do your parents ever come back to visit?"

"They're supposed to come back for Christmas this year. I think they have too much fun travelling around in their motor home like they're gypsies." He chuckles, then turns to Tabby. "We came by to see if we could steal Ruby. The festival is a prime opportunity for theft. We've been patrolling around, keeping an eye on things, and thought she might like to contribute."

"Yes, please," I say before Tabby can answer for me. "I need to change." I disappear into the back of the tent. This will be perfect. I can keep an eye out on people's feet.

Yesterday, Paige and I went over the tapes again. Even though the visual wasn't the best, it was easy to see that the shoes themselves were cheaply made. Whoever is stealing is obviously doing so for money, i.e., because they don't have any. Following that train of thought, it probably won't be easy for them to obtain new shoes or even laces right away. So, they could be walking around either without laces or still using the frayed one. It won't be easy to spot, but it's something to look for. Along with the canvas bags.

The only problem is that I really don't want to be around Jared. Not because he's an ass, but because he's no longer an ass.

Once concealed behind the flap of the tent, I take a deep breath and start removing the costume, which quickly proves to be a problem. I forgot about the ties in the back. I struggle for a moment, but there's no way I'm getting this thing off without untying it.

I stick my head out of the hole to ask Tabby to help me, but she's talking to a customer in a large cowboy hat, explaining the benefits of a lure used to catch some kind of sea bass.

Troy is on his cell phone about ten feet away from the booth, his back facing me.

"Troy," I call out to him anyway.

He turns, sees me, and then points at his phone, rolls his eyes and points at Jared.

"I need help," I say, ignoring his silent commands.

I really don't want to ask Jared for help, but Troy waves me off and turns around again, away from me.

I can't exactly ignore Jared. He's standing near Troy, hands on hips, brows raised in my direction. He totally saw that whole exchange. I can continue to try to squirm myself out, or I can pull myself together and just ask him.

"Will you help me untie this thing?" I ask, gesturing toward my back with my fingers. I'm starting to get a little claustrophobic, especially after Troy talked about sweating all over the inside of the costume.

Unfortunately, Jared nods and joins me in the back of the tent.

It's suddenly much smaller in the enclosure than it was a moment ago.

I turn my back to him. "Tabby tied it for me earlier," I say, although I have no idea what that has to do with anything or why he should care who tied it. All he has to do is untie it. I press my lips together to avoid any more nonsense from erupting.

The fabric tightens for a moment against my skin as he works the ribbons apart.

I wait for the costume to loosen around me, but it seems to take forever.

And then his fingers brush against my bare skin, making my skin tingle and shooting goose bumps up my back. I draw in a short, shallow breath.

"Sorry," he murmurs. "She really tied this in a knot."

It takes a few more seconds of tugging and warm fingers brushing against my skin before the costume finally sags around me and I hold it up without turning around.

"Thanks."

The tent flap jostles as he leaves without saying a word.

I take a minute to gather my breath and get changed, feeling hotter without the costume than I did in it.

Once I'm back in my normal jeans and T-shirt, I meet Troy and Jared out in front of the booth.

"We should split up," Jared says.

"Right. Troy and I can check the perimeter and work our way in." It's a bit bossy of me, but I really don't want to spend more time with Jared and I'm not going to examine that reluctance too closely.

Troy lifts a brow at me and Jared frowns slightly, but then nods in agreement. "I'll go from the center out and meet you guys in the middle."

We split and I can breathe again.

"Come on, Ruby me dear." Troy takes my arm and we meander through the crowd toward the outer booths. "Tell me if you see any ghosts or aliens or anything. And also why you're avoiding Jared like he's got a flesh-eating parasite."

"I'm not avoiding anyone."

"You can't fool me. You like him, don't you? I'm totally telling him."

"Troy!"

"I will make you regret ever deciding to spend time with me."

"Too late."

He laughs and thankfully drops the whole Jared thing.

We spend a couple of hours walking around looking for trouble, but everyone seems to be having a great time. I keep an eye out for people with the canvas bags and cheap shoes, but it's not very effective.

The festival is more diverse than I expected. There are

booths with clothes, food, artwork, all kinds of items I never would have thought of at a Bike, Fish, and Cookie Festival. But they do all have bikes, fish, or cookies on them. Except the booths with carnival-type games, and the funnel cake which Troy buys for me after I tell him I've never had it in my life.

"You've never had funnel cake?" he says, his voice incredulous.

"Never. It's amazing." I shove a big bite in my mouth and chew. I'll have to save some for Paige. She's supposed to be coming here after school lets out. I check my watch. School's been over for twenty minutes so she should be around here any time now.

"Didn't you ever go to a state fair or anything when you were a kid?"

"My parents never had time to take us," I say. Which is the truth. We never stayed anywhere long enough that I could go, and carnivals really weren't their thing; there was no money in it. We spent most of our time pretending to have more money than we actually did at swanky country clubs and charity dinners. Those were my parents' hunting grounds. Where pockets were deep and morality was low.

"What did they do?" he asks.

"Um . . ." I take another big bite of the powdered-sugar-covered confection to give myself some time to formulate a response. "They worked a lot of different jobs." I shrug. "We moved around a lot." All very true.

We stop at a few booths and Troy checks in with the people working to make sure they haven't had any thefts or seen anything unusual. No one has anything to report. We stumble across the boys we bought Gravy from, Gary and Greg, at one of the booths, playing some game where you shoot a water gun into the big mouth of a fish and win prizes.

And we finally run into Paige with her new friend, Naomi.

"Can I stay the night at Naomi's tonight? Please?" Paige begs after I hand her the remaining half of my funnel cake.

Naomi is a sweet-looking girl with dark hair and big eyes that are also pleading in my direction.

"As long as it's okay with her parents."

"I live with my grandma. My dad's overseas in the military," Naomi tells me.

"Okay, well as long as it's okay with Grandma. I should probably meet her." I scrunch my face. Is that how this works? We've never done something as formal as a sleepover.

Actually, I'm not sure I've ever spent even one full night away from Paige, unless you count the one drunken night at Tabby's, but even then I apparently couldn't handle being without her.

Troy, of course, knows her. "Mrs. Andrews," he says. "She's a cool lady. Paige will be fine." He offers me a disarming smile.

"Come home first before you go," I tell Paige. I'll go with her then to meet the grandma.

Then I let her and her friend wander off to do whatever it is teenage girls do.

Troy pats me on the arm while I'm watching them walk away. "You're doing a good job. She's a good kid."

I smile up at him, relieved. "Thanks."

Although if he knew the truth . . .

We walk around a little bit more and then meet up with Jared at Tabby's booth when most of the vendors are starting to pack up.

"Well, this was a bust," Troy says after Jared confirms his afternoon was the same as ours—uneventful.

"Did you get anything?" Jared asks me.

I shake my head.

"You guys gonna stay and help me pack up?" Tabby asks.

"I have a lot of very important police work to do," Troy says, backing away. "This town is counting on me to avenge them, protect them from evil forces, fight for justice and the American way."

"You're ridiculous," Tabby calls after him, but he's already turned to jog away.

"I have real work to do," Jared says. "Finishing up the paperwork from the gas station, still."

Tabby shakes her head. "You're both lying liars who lie."

"I'll help you," I tell her after Jared has waved his goodbyes and stalked off after Troy.

She wraps an arm around my shoulders with a sigh. "You're my only hope."

I laugh. "I don't have anything to do until later anyway. Paige is having her first sleepover at Naomi's." I grimace.

"Uh-oh," she says. "That frown is bad. Baby's first night out? We should do something to distract you."

I definitely don't want to end up at the bar again. But a distraction sounds divine. I don't want to think about Paige being gone, or Jared, or the fact that there's a ticking clock and I probably won't see any of these people in T minus three months and counting.

"Do you want to come over and watch movies or something?" I suggest.

Her eyes light up. "Yes! Girls' night! I'll bring the booze and the nail polish."

"Nail polish?"

"Okay, so it's been a while since I hung out and did the whole girly thing, like sixteen years, but still, I don't think things have changed."

I've never had a girls' night at anyone's house, so I guess I'll have to go along with whatever she's saying.

As long as it doesn't involve Jared or playing psychic, I'm in.

Chapter Fifteen

TABBY SHOWS up right as I'm leaving to drop Paige off at Naomi's.

"Sorry," I tell Tabby. "We're running late. Naomi lives on the other block, so I'll be right back. Go ahead and make yourself at home."

Tabby nods and walks past us into the house. "Groovy. I'll get the margaritas sorted." She's carrying a couple of plastic bags. "Do you have a blender?"

"It's in the bottom cabinet by the fridge," I call after her.

Naomi's grandmother is nice but tries to talk to me for way too long. By the time I'm running up to my door, I'm worried Tabby will be mad I left her for so long.

I'm rushing so much, I don't even notice the figure on the roof.

"I've been thinking," Tabby calls down.

"Did you have to get up on my roof to do that?"

"I could probably fix this for you," she says. "I could bring over some supplies to get it patched up. I'd only charge you for materials."

I gape up at her. "You already got me the display case."

She shrugs. "That's what friends are for," she calls before disappearing from view.

A few seconds later she comes around the side of the house with a ladder.

"Where'd you get that?" I ask.

"Mr. Bingel." She gives me a cheeky grin.

"He talked to you?"

"Sort of. I asked him to borrow the ladder and he grunted and complained but then unlocked his garage before stomping back inside."

We laugh.

An hour later we're in the living room with green mud covering our faces, something that Tabby assured me would shrink pores, watching *Legally Blonde* and eating ice cream straight from the carton.

"I've always wanted to do this," Tabby says.

"Do what?"

"Girly stuff with other girls. It's no fun when you already know everyone in town and they suck. I've had a girls' night with Troy, but it's not the same."

I try to picture it. "You got Troy to do a mud mask?"

"Oh yeah, more than once. He always complains but I think he secretly loves it. Especially when we give each other pedicures."

That mental image makes me laugh. "You could do these things with Eleanor."

Tabby makes a face. "She's nice, but she's so boring."

"Maybe she's shy."

"You're right. I bet she's a freaky wildcat underneath those cashmere cardigans. She probably has whips and chains and a cage under her bed."

I cringe, an image of her and Jared popping involuntarily into my head.

There's an unfamiliar churning in my stomach when I think about Jared, and when I think about Jared with Eleanor.

"Maybe Jared likes those things," I say out loud, fishing for a little more information.

"I don't think Jared is into her like that, although Mrs. Olsen sure does try. She's been working on Jared ever since he moved back. Lucky for him, there aren't many single women in his age range. Or unlucky, depending on how you look at it." She pauses and eyes me speculatively. "Although you're here now. His pool has widened."

"Jared doesn't like me," I say quickly.

"That's not true."

"How do you know?"

"Because he likes everyone."

"That's a terrible answer."

"It's true though. He comes across as a turd-nugget sometimes if you don't know him, but inside he's like a giant marshmallow."

"Hardly." I know, I've felt that hard chest.

"I'm telling you, it's true. I've known him a long time."

We're silent for a moment. The ice cream has been demolished and now we're munching on buttery popcorn and sipping our margaritas while Reese Witherspoon wins her case because of a bad perm.

"I heard you and Jared ran into the Newsomes up in the woods," Tabby says.

"Yes." I grin at her, making the nearly dry mud mask crack on my face. "They were naked."

She laughs. "You're kidding."

I grimace. "I only wish I were. My retinas are permanently scarred."

"I knew the whole break-up thing with them was bullshit. They like to play games with each other."

"I guess that's one way to keep the romance alive," I muse. "Speaking of romance, what's going on with you and Ben?"

"What? Who? Nothing."

"I know you guys hook up all the time."

A slow red hue creeps up her neck. "We do not hook up." She won't meet my eyes. Instead, she shoves a handful of popcorn in her mouth and chews loudly.

"You're a terrible liar."

She finishes her chewing and takes a drink of her margarita before saying, "Having a psychic friend is really cramping my style."

"I don't have to be psychic to know there's something going on there."

"It's possible we maybe sometimes share a little, teensy-weensy, no-big-deal, I-kiss-my-grandmother-with-this-mouth kind of kiss," she relents, but adds, "It doesn't mean anything."

"Are you sure? It's obvious he's into you."

She snorts. "Right, he's into me like people are into the DMV."

"The other night, he seemed pretty upset when Mrs. Olsen mentioned Jack. Who is Jack, by the way?"

"He's a guy who works at the store sometimes." She waves me off. "Mrs. Olsen has lost her damn mind. Jack is like eighteen. I'm old enough to be his . . . much older sister."

"I don't think Ben agrees. He didn't seem happy."

"Ben and I are never going to happen. He doesn't like me like that, we'll never be more than occasional make-out buddies, he will never take it any further, and we are never ever getting together. Like ever."

"Why?"

She's quiet for a moment. Her gaze is on the TV but I don't think she's really watching. When she speaks again, she's more serious than I've ever heard her. "We're friends. We've known each other since we were in diapers, and he's Troy's best friend. If we did take it to the next level and things didn't work out, we wouldn't be able to escape each other. It would make it weird for everyone."

"That sounds like the lamest excuse I've ever heard."

"It is. But it's his excuse, not mine."

I wince. "Ouch."

She shrugs.

"What's your excuse?"

"I can't be with someone who doesn't love me as much as I love them." The words come out easily, almost as if they don't matter, but I can tell they do.

I'm not sure if there's anything I could do to help her, but I want to try.

"Here." I hold my hand out. "Let me see your palm."

"What? No." She smacks my hand away. "I don't want you to do your voodoo shit on me."

"Stop being ridiculous. You've been begging for my voodoo shit for days. Now hold my hand."

She puts her hand in mine. "I've been waiting for you to ask to hold hands since we first met."

"Stop being creepy or I won't rub your feet later."

She snorts a laugh.

I examine the lines for a moment before speaking. "Your heart line has an offshoot. See here?" I point. I have learned some things from all my psychic book reading. "This means that you have a choice. One path will lead to this little, weak line that tapers off into nothing. This other line is longer and deeper."

"Longer and deeper, huh?" She starts laughing, her shoulders shaking, her palm twitching in mine. "I definitely want the guy that can go *longer and deeper*." She snorts.

"Stop laughing. This isn't funny. I didn't mean it like that!" I smack her on the shoulder.

She pulls her hand back. "Okay, Yoda, I get it, choose wisely, don't sleep with the weak ones, yadda yadda yadda."

"What if Ben is your longer and deeper?"

Her laughter subsides and she gives me a sad smile. "It doesn't matter, if I'm not his."

Chapter Sixteen

THE NEXT MORNING, I'm home alone making coffee when I hear a thump at the door. I startle and Gravy hisses at me from his perch on the counter.

"How is it my fault someone is out there?" I ask the cat as I walk past him.

He stares without blinking, jumps off the counter, and flicks his tail at me before disappearing into the living room. He moves pretty smoothly for a cat missing a leg.

The porch is empty.

I talked to Paige thirty minutes ago and she won't be home for another hour.

The floorboards squeak underneath as I approach the stairs leading down to the walkway. At the top of the steps, I lean forward to peer around the bushes lining the front of the house.

"Gary?"

He's sitting on the lawn in front of the neglected rose-bushes. He's even scruffier than the last time I saw him.

"Are you okay?"

He nods. "I wanted to check on Gravy." His face is so small and sad.

"You can come see Gravy any time you want."

"I can?" He gazes up at me, eyes almost as big as his face.

"Sure. He's inside, I think in the living room. Come on."

His eyes widen even further, and a grin spreads across his small face as he scrambles to his feet and follows me into the house.

We find Gravy in a sunny spot on the living room floor, rolling around and exposing his belly. Until he sees me.

Gary kneels next to him and pets him, and Gravy doesn't hiss. The bastard actually purrs.

"Stupid cat," I grumble from the doorway.

"What?"

"Nothing. Would you like something to eat? I was going to make some pancakes."

I wasn't, but the child has that hungry look about him. It might be a boy thing.

"Okay," he says, not turning around, his attention focused on Gravy.

A few minutes into the pancake flipping, Gary ends up in the kitchen. That damn cat is even letting Gary hold him, all awkward and three legs akimbo, and Gravy doesn't fight it, just lounges there limply like he's not the antichrist.

"Gravy really likes you," I say. "He likes Paige, too, but I'm not sure if he likes her enough to let her hold him like that. You're very lucky."

Gary nods and sets Gravy down gently on the floor before sitting at the table.

I flip a few pancakes onto a plate and set them in front of him with a small bottle of syrup.

"Do you want some orange juice?"

Another nod.

I get everything in front of him and watch as he practically shovels the food in his mouth.

While he's eating, I use up the remaining batter.

When all is said and done, the small child eats six decent-sized pancakes.

"Can I bring some to my brother?" he asks, eyeing the remaining food.

"Sure. Where is Greg?"

"He's sleeping. He wasn't feeling good. But maybe this will make him feel better."

"Pancakes cure all sorts of sickness."

That perks him up almost more than Gravy. "You think so?"

"Absolutely. If he's doing better, you guys can come back later today. We're having a grand opening and there will be food and a bounce house and lots of people." Apparently, Tabby's young employee has a bounce house that his parents bought. He agreed to come over and set it up for us.

"Really?" His eyes widen. "We can come?"

"Sure. Your dad can come, too."

At the mention of his father, his expression turns pensive. "He's not feeling well either."

He's lying. I know it. Instead of pushing him, I change the subject.

"The opening isn't until later in the afternoon, because of the festival, but if you come over by two or three, that would be good. We'll have a lot of people around and plenty to eat and some fun things to do."

He seems excited about that, so I pack the leftover pancakes along with a couple of apples into a small paper bag and Gary leaves to check with his brother. I watch as he disappears out of sight around the next block.

While I'm still standing out front, Tabby pulls up in an old pickup truck full of crap. Troy and Jared are with her.

"I thought I'd bring some extra muscle," she tells me when they all exit the vehicle and start unloading tools and tiles and other various items.

"Tabby, we're not remodeling, we're just doing a little cooking and cleaning. We don't need all this stuff."

"Oh I know, but there's another storm system moving in next weekend and I wanted to get your roof fixed so you don't get more water. Mold is the last thing you want, trust me."

I open my mouth to argue but she stops me with a hand.

"It won't take very long. Troy and I will work on the roof and Jared can help you with the last-minute stuff for the shop."

My stomach somersaults. I haven't been alone with Jared since the break-in at the gas station and his big apology. Since he started being all nice and weird.

The shop is set up with everything we need, but we still need to make some appetizers and such for the opening. I spent a good chunk of the check from the police on the food, and I hope it's worth it.

"Any progress on the case?" I ask Jared once we're both doing something, me chopping vegetables while he throws some fake cheese into a Crock-Pot for a dip.

I never said it was fancy food.

"Nope. It's like this guy is a ghost."

"Maybe it's a girl."

"Could be."

He turns on the Crock-Pot and leans against the counter

next to me. "There's no sign of forced entry at the gas station, and the only two people with keys are the owner and the manager. The owner has no reason to destroy his own property, and the manager was out of town on the night of the break-in."

"Maybe the owner wanted insurance money?"

Jared chuckles. "Billy wouldn't know the first thing about insurance fraud."

We're silent for a moment, the only sound the knife hitting the cutting board as I chop.

"Have you—"

"What do you—"

We both laugh a bit awkwardly. "You first," I say.

"Have you had any more . . . I don't know what you call them, visions?"

"No."

He nods and we resume our silent cooking.

"What were you going to say, before?" he asks.

"I was wondering what there is to do around here, for fun."

He eyes me speculatively. "Like what kind of fun?"

"I mean, with Paige. I wanted to take her somewhere fun for kids."

"Oh. Well, there's a movie theater downtown, but they usually only have one or two things playing at any given time and they're usually already available on DVD. The drive-in should be opening soon, too. That's a little ways outside of town. There's also a zoo of sorts, an animal rescue place about an hour south."

I frown. That's too bad. Paige loves animals. "Anything within walking distance?"

"Why within walking distance?"

"Our car is broken. I haven't had a chance to get it fixed with everything that's been going on."

"Do you want me to take a look at it?"

"No," I say firmly.

"You could borrow my car for a few hours if you need to. Anytime."

"I couldn't impose on you like that."

And I wouldn't want to be any more indebted to the people around here than I already am. Plus, offering a handout is almost offensive. Like I can't take care of Paige and our needs on my own, when I totally can.

Although I didn't react this strongly when Tabby gave me stuff. With Jared, it's different.

"It wouldn't be an imposition."

"It's fine," I say, my voice a little more terse than intended. "I'm sure after today things will slow down a bit and we can get the car running."

And I can get the money to get it fixed.

We're quiet after that, no chitchat other than what's necessary to hand each other utensils and get everything arranged on platters or in the oven.

Paige comes home and helps us in the kitchen. She seems tired but happy from her sleepover. It sounds like she and Naomi had an evening similar to mine and Tabby's, minus the margaritas.

We've finished stacking trays into the refrigerator for later when a small voice interrupts us.

"Miss Ruby?"

I turn around at the sound of the voice.

Gary is back, standing in the doorway, and he brought his older brother this time.

Greg doesn't exactly seem enthused to be here. I wonder if he's still not feeling well. He has gray smudges under his eyes, and he's paler than the last time I saw him at the festival.

"Hey, Gary. You came back a bit early."

"Did you guys want to hang out and wait for the bounce house?" Paige asks them.

They both perk up at that.

She leads them outside, Gravy trailing after them.

"Will you help me get the pitcher down?" I ask Jared, pointing to the top of a tall cabinet. "I can bring some lemonade outside. I'm sure Tabby and Troy need a break by now."

Jared nods and reaches up over me, grabbing the glass pitcher and setting it on the counter. The kids left the front door open and I can hear Troy yelling something about a football.

By the time Jared and I make it out front to see what the noise is all about, Troy has all three kids, including Paige, set up on the front lawn and he's showing them the proper way to line up and tackle.

"You're my offensive line," he tells Paige.

"By myself?" She does not sound impressed.

I set the pitcher of lemonade and glasses down on the front stoop and Tabby bounces up the steps, pouring herself a glass and taking a few big swallows. She's still got a tool belt wrapped around her waist. She looks like Home Improvement Barbie.

"We fixed up the bad spots for now, and that should last you through the summer, but you'll probably need an entirely new roof next year," Tabby tells me. "We should look into metal. It lasts longer in the harsh seaside climate."

Next year. I won't be here next year.

I shove that thought aside.

Almost everything is ready for the opening and now I don't have to worry about the roof leaking any more than it already has.

"Thank you," I tell her, but she waves off my appreciation and stalks off to the truck to unload her belt.

Jared sits on the porch swing next to me and we watch the boys and Paige play.

Gravy decides he's in love with Jared and rolls around at his feet, exposing his stomach. And when Jared bends over to pet his soft underbelly, Gravy purrs.

"What is this?" I can't help but say, gesturing to the beast. "This cat loves everyone but me."

"Where'd you get him?"

"I bought him from Greg and Gary."

He nods. "They seem like good kids. I think they're pretty new in town. I don't recognize them."

We sit on the porch in silence for a few moments before Jared speaks again. "It's nice of you to spend time with them." He's still scratching Gravy's belly, but he looks up at me when he's finished speaking, his dark eyes appearing brighter in the sun.

I squirm under his gaze. "It's no big deal."

A grumbling on the side of the house catches my attention. It's Mr. Bingel, out in his yard getting ready to trim his already perfect rosebushes that he was just out here trimming this morning.

He pretends like he doesn't notice us, but it's impossible to miss Troy roaring on the ground, covered in laughing children trying to get him to drop the football.

I have to laugh.

This is what I've been missing. The kids on the lawn, sitting on a porch swing, drinking lemonade in the sunshine. I wish all life could be as simple as this.

"Hey, Jim," Jared calls out when he spots Mr. Bingel. He stands up and ventures over onto Mr. Bingel's side of the yard.

My mouth drops. I've never crossed the invisible line. I'm pretty sure I'd get my head clipped off with Mr. Bingel's shears.

But Mr. Bingel doesn't seem to mind Jared's presence as much as mine, even though he's still scowling. They shake hands and talk, but I can't hear their conversation over the giggles and chatter on the lawn in front of me.

"Hey." Tabby sits in the space Jared vacated.

"Tabby, thanks for doing all of this. I really appreciate it."

"Not a problem. We help each other around here. Next time I need a psychic prediction, I expect you to return the favor."

"Absolutely."

We sit on the porch and watch Troy, who now has a boy on the end of either arm while he spins them in circles and Paige looks on and claps.

"Whose rug rats?" Tabby asks, taking a sip of lemonade.

"I'm not really sure. Their names are Greg and Gary. I bought Gravy from them."

"That's a whole lot of G names," she says, scratching her head.

"Did you see that Mr. Bingel is talking to Jared?" I ask her in a low voice, leaning a little toward her so they won't hear.

She peers around my new porch banister and watches them for a second. "Crazy. Mr. Bingel is actually talking, and not just spewing insults. Well, not shocking exactly. Everyone in this town loves Jared. And I bet despite his grumblings, Mr. Bingel actually wants someone to talk to."

I'm sure he does. And he still looks stiff in the hips. He's probably too proud to ask someone for help, but . . . Standing, I wipe my hands on my shorts. I really hope this doesn't blow up in my face.

"Greg, Gary," I call out.

Troy is lying on the lawn, pretending sleep, while the boys tug on his arms and try to wake him up and Paige pulls on one of his legs. The boys stop when I call out their names.

I motion for them to follow me across the lawn.

Mr. Bingel eyes the boys as if they are feral dogs that might bite, and for a second I waver. What if this is a bad idea?

But I have the boys standing next to me, their shoddy clothes apparent in the bright light of the late afternoon, and I have to at least try.

"Hey, Mr. Bingel."

Instead of returning the greeting, he scowls. But I think that's an improvement; there's no talk about idiot girls or other insults.

"This is Gary and Greg. They're helping me with some chores and odd jobs to help earn a little cash. Is there anything you need help with around your house?"

I take a breath and wait. This could go one of two ways. One, he says no and he goes back to pretending I don't exist and insulting me under his breath. Or two, he could actually take this opportunity to help a couple of struggling kids. He would have some company, maybe his arthritic hip could take a rest, and then maybe his attitude would also improve.

Having Jared standing there might actually work to my

advantage, because Mr. Bingel glances over at him before peering down at the boys over the top of his glasses.

"Well, now. I might have some things that they can help me out with. Why don't you boys come over after school on Monday?"

They both quickly nod and agree to come back, their voices full of "thank you sir."

I can't help but grin.

Jared meets my eyes over the boys' heads as they talk to Mr. Bingel.

He smiles at me. The big kind of smile that crinkles the eyes and makes his whole face light up.

My heart does a somersault.

I'm in so much trouble.

Chapter Seventeen

THE REST of the afternoon moves swiftly. A guy shows up to set up the bounce house, the kids help with some finishing touches, sweeping and the like, and I barely have time to run inside and shower off the dust and grime before customers start arriving.

I find a long skirt that Ruby must have left behind that looks sufficiently bohemian, and I pair it with a plain white T-shirt. I put my hair up and frown at myself in the mirror. My roots are growing out, but there's no hope for it. It's not like I can run over to the salon and get it fixed.

I have to take a moment to breathe deeply and try to remember why I'm doing this. I've been going through the books in the shop, and I think I have enough canned phrases to make it through some quick readings. Really, it's just like any other con, but with the added layer of mysticism thrown in for giggles.

When I get downstairs, it's not three yet, but people are already in line and Paige is taking their money at the register and writing all their names down on a list.

"We'll call your name when it's your turn," she's yelling over the line of people. "First come, first serve, and we're shutting down by nine."

"Paige," I get her attention from the doorway.

She comes loping over. "I already have five hundred bucks. Some of these people are giving me more than ten dollars and I told them I can't make change." She grins at her own ingenuity.

"Paige, no taking advantage."

She raises a skeptical brow at that.

"No taking more advantage than we already are," I clarify in a whisper.

I feel bad enough as it is. Sure, we need enough money to blow town in a few months, and this psychic shtick is harmless compared to the stuff we used to do with Mom and Dad. But running cons on people we know and like just feels . . . uncomfortable. Maybe I can inject these "readings" with legitimate advice. Or *some*thing.

"Whatever." She rolls her eyes. "Let me know when you're ready and I'll start sending people into the reading room. Tabby let us borrow her kitchen timer." She hands me a circular white timer, the kind with a screw knob.

I take it and glance around the shop. There's more of a crowd than I expected. People are perusing the books and other items Ruby has for sale. I see Tabby. She changed into a short skirt and a low-cut top. She's bending over in front of Ben to show him something, making the top dip even further and Ben impossibly flustered, which makes me smile.

Amid the throng of blue-hairs, I recognize Mrs. Olsen and Miss Viola, who's asleep in her wheelchair.

I don't have time to stand around though. I tell Paige to go ahead and start and then I go to the reading room and light the candles and wait.

My first ten customers are elderly women, including Mrs. Olsen. Her main concern is getting "all these stupid young people" to hook up. I try to hint to her about Tabby and Ben, but for some reason she doesn't take that bait.

Getting people involved in their reading is the easy part. First, I ask them what they want to know about. This information alone is telling. If someone is concerned about their career, I can tell them they have a promotion or a change in circumstance coming their way. For most people I've met throughout my life, it's either about love or money. Or both. But Castle Cove is different. Most of the people I talk to have already had their great love, and they no longer work, so the career angle is out.

I'm surprised to discover that a majority of them are more interested in hearing information and reassurances about their family than about themselves, although there is the occasional more personal concern.

"I want to know if my son is going to get divorced."

"Will my granddaughter go to college?"

"Will this rash ever go away?"

I keep the predictions or insights vague—using terms that can apply to everyone, like, "Your son has a great deal of untapped capacity that he could use to his advantage."

I also put a positive spin on it. "He's going to be successful, eventually. As long as he moves past his insecurities." It helps that this is what people *want* to hear. It makes it easier for them to accept it as truth.

I don't see any canvas bags or frayed shoelaces, but I do talk to Mrs. Hale, the cupcake thief. In the video, I only saw her from behind, but she always wore funky hats, like she was going to a royal wedding or something. Today is no exception; the hat she has on matches her suit. It's bright blue, and a waterfall of fake silk flowers cascades from the brim.

"My husband, George, was a wonderful man," she tells me. She hasn't really asked for any information at all, more content to talk to me about whatever.

"You were married a long time," I say, deciding to phrase the sentence as a statement instead of a question to make it seem like I know, instead of what I'm really doing, which is fishing.

"Nearly sixty years. I used to bake for him, you know. He had a big sweet tooth." She laughs.

I smile and nod, feeling slightly ashamed about the whole accusing-her-of-theft thing.

"The day he died, he wanted me to make him some chocolate chip cookies. They were his favorite. But I was too busy." She frowns a little and looks down at her hands. She has matching blue gloves. "He wasn't mad. He was always so easygoing, nothing ever got him riled up, and if it did, I knew it was serious. Now I wish I had made him the cookies." She sighs. "He died that night in his sleep. You just never know what's going to happen in life," she says, raising her eyes to mine. "Don't forget that." She reaches out and pats my hand. "If someone you love wants cookies, even if you don't want to make them, you should."

I fleetingly wonder if making cookies is a euphemism for something else, but I shove that thought aside. Obviously Mrs. Hale feels guilty about not making cookies the day George died. No wonder she brings him cupcakes every day.

"I'm sure George understood that you loved him." I cover her hand with my own. "It's plenty clear to me."

That makes her smile.

Chapter Eighteen

THE GRAND OPENING is a major success. We sell a lot of product in addition to making bank on the readings, and I make note of the bestselling items so we can order more and keep track for Ruby when she returns. Even though we won't be here then, at least we can leave her with a little head start on the shop since we're already using her enough.

It's so busy that I barely see Tabby, Troy, or Jared throughout the whole thing until they're leaving. By then, I'm so wiped I can't do more than tell them thank you and goodbye. Tabby gives me a hug, Troy pats me on the back, and Jared waves from a distance as he helps Mrs. Hale into his Jeep to take her home.

Paige and I are exhausted though, and we spend most of Sunday alternating vegging out and cleaning up the leftover mess.

It's on Monday, after I walk her to school, that I come home to find legs sticking out from underneath the frame of our car.

I walk over and stand next to the legs. Waiting.

Eventually, Jared rolls out from under the vehicle.

"Hey." He shades his eyes from the morning sun. "What's up?"

"What are you doing?"

"Fixing the car."

"I told you I don't need your help."

He sits up on the rolling contraption and frowns up at me. "You let Tabby help you with the roof and stuff. Why can't I help you?"

Why indeed?

"Because . . ." I start, but I really don't have a good excuse. "Why do you want to help me, anyway?"

He wipes his hands on a dirty rag and as his arms flex, I try to ignore how sexy his shoulders look in the gray tank top he's wearing.

"Why not?" He doesn't wait for me to answer that question. "Hey, hand me that socket wrench, would you?" He leans down and rolls back under the car.

With a huff, I find the wrench and hand it to him.

I can't have a conversation with his feet, so I give up and go inside.

By the time I finish moping around inside and come to the humbling realization that I'm being a complete ninny, Jared seems to be done under the car. I bring out some ice-cold water as a peace offering, and he chugs it down in a few quick gulps.

"I changed your oil and installed a new battery."

I swallow back my pride. "Thank you."

That makes him smile, his eyes crinkling at the corners. "You're welcome." He hands me the keys. "Let's see if she starts."

The car starts. I try to tell him I'll pay him back but he changes the subject. After Jared leaves, a shipment comes in. It's a bunch of crystals and unicorn figurines. They're individually wrapped and have to be handled with care. I'm bringing in the last box when Gary and Greg walk by, heading toward Mr. Bingel's house.

"Hey." I put the box back down. The boys are covered in mud up to their knees. "What happened to you guys?"

Gary looks up at Greg and he answers for them. "We were walking home from school and got caught up in some mud."

"I can see that. Do you want to come in and clean your-selves up?" Mr. Bingel will freak out if they come into his house covered in muck.

They hesitate, glancing at each other again.

I need a bribe. "You can see Gravy. And I'll make some lemonade."

That seals the deal.

They run up into the house, backpacks bouncing on their shoulders. "Do you have extra clothes?" I ask once we're inside.

Greg shakes his head. His shaggy hair flops about. These boys need haircuts more than I do.

"Only shoes," he says.

"Well, you'll have to clean up as much as you can."

I show the boys the bathroom and laundry room.

"You should probably rinse off the shoes and then throw them in the dryer," I suggest. "It will be faster that way."

I have some cookies leftover from the festival and I pull these out along with the lemonade.

Greg and Gary make quick work of the cookies. They even

eat the oatmeal ones, not being as particular as Tabby is, apparently.

"Did you tell your dad about how you're helping Mr. Bingel?"

Greg nods.

"I think I would like to meet your dad. Where do you guys live?"

"He works a lot. But I'll tell him. I think our clothes are dry. Come on, Gary."

Gary is on the floor, petting Gravy, but when Greg speaks, he stands and they both head down the hall to the laundry room.

Point taken. Greg does not want to talk about his father. I can totally understand that, but I wish they would open up to me.

Maybe their dad is the violent type, but I haven't noticed any bruises or flinching. Maybe he's one of those non-present parents; too drunk or drugged up to care so they're mostly alone. That scenario makes the most sense. Should I tell Jared? No, I can't do that. Jared seems like he genuinely cares, but a cop is a cop. He'd report them to CPS and they'd end up in foster care, which would be worse than being on their own. And they'd probably be separated. At least this way they have each other. They seem to be doing okay. Happy, healthy, still in school. Just perpetually hungry and dirty. And selling three-legged cats. And refusing to answer simple questions about their living situation. But those are typical boy things, right?

Okay, maybe not. Indecisiveness shifts through me. I'll just do whatever I can to help them.

They both thank me for the cookies and lemonade and I watch them head over to Mr. Bingel's.

Paige comes home and we finish unpacking the figurines and putting them in the display case. By the time we're done, the sun is setting, casting pink and orange shots of color through the sky.

While Paige is upstairs doing her homework, I hear children laughing outside and peek out the window in time to see Greg and Gary leaving Mr. Bingel's, their backpacks slung over their shoulders and their arms full of small boxes.

I step outside to see how it went.

"Did you guys help out a lot? How did it go?" I ask, meeting them at the end of the sidewalk.

"Yes. He gave us lots of food." Gary holds up his boxes, which I see now are reusable plastic containers full of food.

"That's nice of him."

"And twenty dollars each," Greg adds, grinning widely.

"That's really something."

I knew it. I knew Mr. Bingel had a heart under the gruff exterior.

"We have to be home before dark," Greg says.

I wait until they disappear around the corner and then I turn toward Mr. Bingel's house. A light comes on in the front room.

It's probably a bad idea. But since I'm full of bad ideas lately, and it doesn't stop me from following through with them, why stop now?

Before I can talk myself out of it, I march up to Mr. Bingel's house and knock on the door.

There's a shuffling from inside before the door swings open.

"Hey, Mr. Bingel," I wave and then immediately wonder

why I made such an awkward gesture when he's standing right in front of me.

His mouth pops open a smidge and he clears his throat and his eyes land anywhere but on me. "What— I— Uh, come in."

Okaaay.

He moves back, opening the door further, and I slowly step over the threshold as if it's a portal into another dimension and I don't want to get sucked in too quickly.

We stand in his living room, staring at everything but each other.

Apparently he doesn't know how to talk unless he's hurling insults from a distance, and I have no idea why I came over here in the first place. I didn't actually expect him to open the door.

Oh, the boys, right.

"Thank you for helping Greg and Gary," I finally say.

He nods. "It's not a problem. They're good boys. It's nice to have children in the house again. Would you like tea?"

He looks as surprised by the offer as I am. As if the words wiggled their way from his mouth without his consent.

"Yes, please," I say before he can retract the offer.

He motions for me to sit.

His living room is small, with wood floors, a thick rug under a small coffee table, and a few chairs. It's clean and well put together though. There are a bunch of pictures cluttered on a side table, but I can't make them out clearly from here.

I sit in one of the chairs and he sits across from me. There's a teapot and cups on a small platter on the table and he pours me a cup. The platter even has a small jar for milk, and sugar cubes in a glass container.

I feel like I'm in Regency England or something.

We go through the motions of taking tea together. I drink mine straight and he drinks his with milk and sugar.

"You said it's nice to have boys in the house *again*," I say, emphasizing the last word.

Mr. Bingel nods. "My son." He tilts his head at the cluster of pictures on the table next to his chair.

I squint at the one he's referring to, but there are too many and I can only see the ones closest to where I'm sitting.

He reaches over, pulls a frame out of the stack, and hands it to me.

I examine the picture closely. The man in the photo is a few years older than me, in a tan uniform with colorful pins adorning his left breast. The United States flag flies in the background.

"What's his name?"

"His name was Jason. He was a marine. Sixth division, twenty-first infantry, Kandahar. He died during a routine supply run. They ran over an IED and . . ." He shrugs.

"I'm sorry."

He takes a sip of his tea and his lips purse. "I would have lost it if it weren't for my wife. We had each other even if we missed Jason so much it was like our chests had been hollowed out. We even talked about adopting or taking care of foster kids. Got screened and on a list and everything. But then she got sick. She died a few years after Jason."

I'm not sure what to say. I already said sorry, and the word is so lacking.

"You only had the one son?" I ask instead.

"Yes. He loved this town. He was the football captain, the prom king. When he was young, there were always children in our house playing, running around. I didn't realize how much I missed it until I heard it again today."

We drink our tea in silence for a moment. Then he says, "Thank you." The words are so soft I almost think I imagine them.

"For what?"

"You suggested they come over here. I never would have done that for myself."

We go back to sipping silently out of our cups again. After a minute, I ask, "Would you like me to pour you some more tea?"

He nods. "Okay."

I leave Mr. Bingel's after an hour of sitting there and listening to him tell stories about how his wife loved to sew and sing old bluegrass songs, and how his son loved the New England Patriots and mowing the law.

When I'm within a few feet of the front door, I hear the phone ringing.

Surprised, I race the rest of the way inside and into the kitchen where the landline is nestled in a cradle, hanging on the wall.

"Hello?" I answer, out of breath.

"Charlotte?" The voice is at once familiar and dreaded.

"Ruby?"

Chapter Nineteen

"Hey girl! How are things going?"

Ruby's voice is happy and bright.

But her question is loaded.

I've taken over your identity. You don't mind, right?

"Things are great," I say. "Everything is coming along as scheduled. The shop is almost ready to go."

"Oh good. I was worried because I got a message that you called a couple of weeks ago? Something about the roof?"

"I've gotten it all taken care of," I rush to explain. Dammit, why did I call her and why did I forget?

"Okay, that's great. So listen, I just got off the phone with my parents, and our accountant is stopping by this week to go over the records you're keeping and check out the shop."

My heart stops in my chest and then restarts in double time. "What?"

"It's not that I don't trust you," she rushes to explain. "I am a people person, Charlotte, and I knew right away that you were good people. I trust you with everything." Her voice is laced with sincerity, and I would think it was sweet if her words weren't so, so stupid.

"It's just that, my parents, you see, I told them I left you in charge of everything, and they started going off on me about how crazy it was to leave a complete stranger in charge of my store." She sounds truly upset. "They never trust my judgment."

"It's fine, Ruby, I understand."

Inside, I'm freaking out. Someone is coming, sometime this week, someone who knows that I'm not Ruby. This whole town thinks I'm Ruby, the friendly psychic that's helping to catch the Castle Cove Bandit. The store is open. We have customers that we shouldn't have. This guy is going to get here and expose me for the fraud that I am.

We're screwed.

"How are things going with the Dalai Lama?" I ask, needing to change the subject to something, anything she can babble about while my mind races.

She rambles on about how she'll be out of reach completely until she leaves, but I'm freaking out too much to pick up much more than that.

What am I going to do?

My brain is a mass of white noise, all of it saying the same thing. *Leave. Get out while you can, before it's too late.*

"So when is this guy coming to check out the store?" I ask brightly when she says she has to hang up.

"I don't know, sometime in the next few days. His name is Jackson Murphy. He's a great guy, you'll love him."

Yeah, as much as I love a needle between my fingers. "That's great. I'll keep an eye out for him. You have fun and don't worry about anything."

"I never do. I know everything will work out great. Talk to you soon, Charlotte!" She clicks off and I'm left holding onto the phone like a lifeline. If I let go, it will all disappear.

~

I don't tell Paige about Ruby's call until the next day when she comes home from school, and I've had a chance to think things over and come up with a plan.

"Okay, here's the deal," I say after she's revived me with coffee and brownies leftover from the opening. I pace back and forth in the living room. "We're going to tell this guy that Ruby said we could open the shop."

One of my many worries. We aren't even supposed to be open yet.

"What if he knows we're not?" Paige asks.

"Even if Ruby talked to him today like I did, she's going to be out of contact until she returns. Which means, for all he knows, I could have talked to her after he did and agreed to open the shop since we have all the merchandise and there's no reason not to. We aren't using that money, so even if he checks, all the receipts will add up."

"Okay, what about the rest of the town?" she asks.

"What do you mean?"

"If anyone comes in looking for a reading, or to buy something while he's here . . ." She grimaces.

"We'll tell everyone we're temporarily closed." I turn around to pace in the opposite direction. We need a reason to keep people away. "We're sick." I snap my fingers. "Or one of us is. One of us has the flu. A bad one. One that will keep everyone away for a few days. I'll be the sick one; you still have to go to school and that way you can spread the word."

"When exactly is he coming?"

Deflated, I plop down next to her on the couch. "She didn't say exactly. Sometime in the next few days."

Paige nods. "I'll start spreading the word tomorrow then." She pats me on the back. "Don't worry. We've been through worse than this." She leans her head against my shoulder.

She ain't lying.

I don't walk Paige to school for the next two days, choosing to spend my time peeking out the window at every sound, wondering when the other shoe is going to drop. Tabby calls and wants to come over for dinner, and I have to tell her about the "flu." She thinks I got sick from touching all those old people's hands during the opening. I ask her to tell Troy so they know I can't help with the investigation for the next couple of days.

Fleetingly, I wonder if we should leave town . . . but while we made enough money from the grand opening to last a couple weeks, there's not enough to find a new place to live and pay rent.

My hope is that this Jackson Murphy guy will show up for a few hours and then leave and I won't have to think of him ever again.

The second day passes, and again, no accountant. The waiting is killing me.

Finally, on the third day—just when I'm starting to feel like Tom Hanks in *Cast Away*, except Wilson isn't a ball, he's a cat named Gravy who still hisses at me constantly and won't let me into the living room—a sleek black sedan pulls into the driveway.

Paige is at school. She shouldn't be home for a couple more hours. Thank god he didn't come by when she was home. One less thing to worry about.

I greet Mr. Murphy at the front door and usher him inside.

Jackson Murphy is younger than I would have thought. In my daydreams, which were more like nightmares, I pictured an older, balding and/or white-haired man with a protruding belly and fancy suit.

He has the fancy suit, but his hair is dark and he can't be more than thirty-five, with a strong jaw and bright blue eyes. He's actually quite attractive, a thought that might be more pressing if I weren't so worried about him ruining my life. His eyes are pretty, sure, but they are also sharp and assessing, which I don't like at all.

After quick introductions, I get right to business.

"When I talked to Ruby a few days ago, we agreed to open the shop, since nearly all the merchandise she purchased has come in."

He stares at me without speaking or smiling, making me nervous.

I clear my throat. "Anyway, I keep all of the records here." I lead him to the checkout counter. "Here's the account ledgers and receipts and invoices that I haven't put into the computer yet." I have all of the paperwork up front at the register. I've gotten everything ready so he can review it and then hopefully get the hell out of here before someone else actually talks to him or I lose my ever-loving mind, whichever happens sooner.

"Can I use the bathroom?" he asks without even a glance at the paperwork I'm holding.

My whole body deflates.

"It's down the hall."

I show him which way to go and then pace the front room, waiting for him to come out. Every creak and movement throughout the house is a jolt to my already-frazzled nerves.

Finally, he comes back, his tie loosened a bit.

"Here's the paperwork," I try again, fairly shoving it in his direction.

"Right. Thanks." He takes the paperwork from me, but instead of reading it, he asks, "Do you have somewhere I can go over this?"

"Sure, sure, you want to go through the paperwork in the kitchen?"

I could bring him upstairs to the office, but I don't want him to get too comfortable and I don't want him to see the live streams of various parts of Castle Cove.

"That sounds great."

He follows me through the house and sits at the small dining table.

I leave him to the numbers and pace the front room, questions zipping through my mind like ping-pong balls. What if he wants to stay the night? No, that's crazy. What if he wants to come back tomorrow? What if he finds something screwy and decides that I'm no good and kicks us out? What if—

"You recorded damages to some of the product. What happened?"

I startle when his voice interrupts my stream of thoughts, then grimace. "My cat," I say. "But I've already ordered replacement products. The invoice should be in there and the product will be here within a couple of weeks. I paid for the replacements with my own funds. That should be listed in there as a credit."

"Does Ruby know you have a pet? I'm not sure animals were allowed in the lease agreement."

"Um. No. I didn't have a cat when I moved here, but there were these kids—"

Uninterested in my explanation, apparently, he interrupts me to keep his line of questioning going.

"You have some notes in here about a leaky roof?"

"Oh. Yes. I had it repaired."

"Do you have an invoice for that?"

"No, a friend of mine . . . um, the owner of the local hardware store came over and repaired it. I paid her back by working for her. But she said the roof will need to be replaced before winter."

He frowns, a crease forming between his brows. "Mm-hmm," he says, making some notes in his phone.

Mm-hmm? What does that mean?

"What about the bed? You had to replace it?"

"Not yet."

"Were there any other damages?"

I shake my head no.

His eyes run down the paper before meeting mine. "I'll have someone deliver a new mattress. Ruby will probably want something that will last and is environmentally friendly."

"Oh, okay."

The thumping of my heart and the sweating of my palms abate for a moment. He doesn't want to kick me out. And it sounds like he's done. I figured it wouldn't take too long, there isn't that much stuff to go through. Maybe he'll leave and everything will be fine.

"Everything else looks in order," he says. "Just keep your cat out of the store, and I think you'll be okay." He smiles.

A wave of relief crashes over me. "Great."

He clicks his briefcase together. "I'll be getting out of your hair then." He hands me a business card. "My numbers are all on there. Don't be afraid to call me if you need anything else that isn't a minor repair."

"I will," I say, a bit in a daze as I walk with him toward the front room.

Before we make it halfway there, a loud knock at the door freezes me midstep.

My heart, which had just started to calm itself, races yet again. Who's at the door? They can't be here, not now, not when Jackson is so close to leaving.

"Are you okay?"

Oh shit, he's still behind me.

"Oh, fine! I'll . . . see who that is."

I wish he wouldn't follow me, but what else is he going to do? He's trying to leave. I can't very well ask him to hide.

This might be the moment where everything falls down around me in a flood of disgrace.

Crossing my fingers that it's just another delivery, I pull open the door.

It's Jared.

Chapter Twenty

HE'S IN HIS UNIFORM, holding some kind of to-go food container.

"Hi," I say.

Oh crap. All my worst nightmares are coming true. If it's discovered I'm a fraud, what will happen to Paige?

"Tabby said you were sick," Jared says. His gaze is fixed somewhere over my shoulder.

"Oh, I, uh, yes. I have been sick."

I have no idea what to say next. I probably don't look sick at all. Then I realize Jared isn't just staring over my shoulder. He's staring at Jackson. I clear my throat around the lump that's formed there. "Jared, this is Jackson Murphy, he's . . ." I have to be very careful about how I word this next sentence. "He's an accountant. Mr. Murphy, this is Jared Reeves, our local deputy."

I force a smile to my face. It will be okay, right? Dear god, don't let Jackson refer to anything about me not being Ruby. Like, calling me by my name or mentioning Ruby at all or really, anything else.

Jackson smiles at Jared. "Just making sure all of Ruby's accounts are in order."

My smile is frozen on my face, my brain not registering the words for a few seconds before analyzing and deeming them safe. Okay. That's okay. It's normal to refer to people in the third person, even when they're standing right there, right?

"He's leaving," I say quickly. I move back to let him pass. "Thank you for everything."

"Thank you," he says. "It was nice to meet you." The words are directed at me, but Jared—probably assuming I had met the accountant before—is the one who responds.

"Nice to meet you, too," he says.

Luckily for me, Jackson smiles and leaves, probably, hopefully, not realizing that Jared didn't realize the words were intended for me and not him.

I can't move or speak until Jackson is safely in his car and backing out of the driveway.

My breath rushes out of my lungs and I finally focus on Jared.

"I brought you some soup." Jared holds up the container.

"That's so nice," I say, taking the dish from him. It's warm in my hands.

He's watching me. Is that glint in his eyes concern or suspicion?

Better to be safe than sorry.

I cough and turn away, putting the container on the shelf nearest me so I can make the coughing fit more convincing. As I cough into my hands, I rub under my eyes to make them a bit watery and red before turning back around.

"Are you sure you're better? You don't look so good."

"I think I just need to sleep some more." I add a grimace and a sway to make the performance more convincing.

"Do you need help?" Jared is next to me, his hand on my arm.

"I'm good. I'm going to sleep. Thanks for the soup, I'll see you later."

His hand is still on my arm, warm and sturdy and reassuring.

"I'm not sure I should leave you like this. At least let me put the soup in the fridge and make sure you get to your bed, okay?"

"Okay, yeah, that's fine." I let him think he's helping me, all the better to convince him of my honesty and general helplessness.

I lean on him while he walks me up to my room.

"Thank you," I sniffle with a yawn while he helps me into bed.

Then I listen to his footsteps track back down the stairs. He shuffles around in the kitchen for a minute before he finally heads out the front door. To be safe, I wait a few extra minutes before going back downstairs myself.

The soup is in the fridge, and there's a note on the counter.

Get some rest. I'll pick up Paige and make sure she has dinner, the note reads.

It's signed *J.*

He's going to take care of Paige for me.

Dumbfounded, I slump against the counter. I'm pulling one over on him, and he's going to take her to dinner. Guilt swarms against my insides like angry kittens with tiny, sharp claws.

What if he's taking her to dinner as a ruse, but he actually knows I'm a big fat liar and he's taking her away to grill her?

I shake my head. No. He totally believed my ruse.

Still. I feel a little anxious, waiting for them to return. I spend the next couple of hours peeking out the front window until his cruiser finally pulls up at the curb.

I race back to the kitchen, fluffing my hair and mussing it with my fingers to make it look like I just woke up.

Throwing the soup container in the microwave, it runs for a few seconds before I hear the front door opening.

"Will you show me how to shoot your gun?" Paige's voice accompanies the clomping of her feet across the hardwood floors as they come into the house through the shop.

"I don't know, we'll have to check with your sister," Jared's rumbling voice follows.

"Hey, you're up," Paige says when she sees me standing in the kitchen. "Are you feeling better?" She gives me a hug and takes the opportunity to whisper in my ear. "He totally bought it."

I give her a relieved smile as she steps back. "I'm feeling much better. Where did you guys go?"

Paige is holding a small pizza box in her hands.

"Jared took me to dinner at JJ's. It's like thirty minutes away, but they have great pizza. We should go sometime."

"Sounds good."

She puts the pizza box in the fridge and then eyes me and Jared in turn. "I have homework." And she disappears down the hall with a quick smile. A second later, her feet pound up the stairs.

"Thanks for taking care of Paige." I turn my back to grab a spoon out of the drawer.

When I turn back around, he's leaning against the doorway, arms crossed over his chest. "She's a good kid."

"I think so." I glance at the ground, uncomfortable with his presence, not really sure why he's still here and what he wants from me. "Um. I'm going to eat this in the living room and watch something girly so . . ." *you are free to leave*, hint hint. I mostly hope he'll take off, but a smaller, yet stronger part of me hopes he'll stay.

"What are you going to watch?" he asks.

What could I say to make him leave?

"I Love Lucy." I walk past him toward the living room. To my surprise and dismay, he follows me.

"I love that show."

"You do?"

"Yeah. My favorite episode is the one where she bought all the baby chicks and they get out everywhere."

"Right. That's a good one," I say, for lack of any better words or turning into a pile of goo at his feet.

I turn the TV on and sit on the couch with my soup. He sits at the opposite end.

We watch the show in silence until I've finished eating.

"Thank you for the soup, it was delicious," I tell him. I lean forward to put the now empty bowl on the table and then sit back, which moves me a couple inches closer to Jared.

"It's no problem."

"Thanks again for fixing the car. And taking care of Paige. And feeding her, and me . . . I'm sorry I was cranky about it earlier. It's just that I'm not used to getting help. It sort of stings to realize I need it."

"Everyone needs a hand sometimes. I didn't mean to imply that you're helpless. It's obvious you've done a great job with

Paige. I didn't exactly make it easy on you when you first got here, and I feel bad about that. I guess what I'm trying to say is that I'm willing to help out if you ever need it."

While he talks, he leans a little in my direction.

I'm not sure what to make of it. I still don't understand why he wants to help me. What is he getting in return?

I take in our positions on the couch, leaning toward each other. I didn't even realize we had been moving closer.

My thoughts turn. What if he does want something in exchange for helping me? It makes more sense than believing anyone would do kind deeds out of the goodness of their hearts. Tabby wants me to be her friend because she has none in town, so she helps me. I get that. I give her someone to hang out with, she gives me cabinets. I help her at the festival, and she fixes my roof. What's Jared's angle?

"I'm not going to sleep with you for fixing my car," I blurt.

His brows lift and he leans back onto the arm of the couch.

"That's not where I thought this was going." He tilts his head, his eyes sharp and assessing. "Haven't you ever had anyone help you without expecting something in return?"

I don't know how to answer that. There are no selfless good deeds, at least not that I've ever experienced.

He doesn't seem to expect a response because he keeps talking.

"I'm not helping you to get something from you. I've seen the way you take care of your sister, and those boys and Mr. Bingel. And Mrs. Hale told me about her reading. You made her feel better about her husband. Something I've been trying and failing to do for years. I'll admit, I don't understand what it is you actually do, but you are making a difference here. I can respect that."

I have no idea how to respond to his barrage of compliments.

Is he for real?

"I guess what I'm trying to say, very badly, is that I like you."

He likes me?

I don't know how to process this. Does this mean he *likes* me, likes me?

He sticks his hand in my direction. "Friends?"

Oh, right.

Friends.

I nod carefully and shake his hand.

His fingers grip mine, warm and stable.

"Friends."

Chapter Twenty-One

I SPEND a few days avoiding Jared and pretty much everyone except for customers and people who come in for readings. Luckily, it's not too busy but steady enough to provide distraction.

I even avoid Tabby because where Tabby and Troy go, Jared is likely to follow. I don't mind being his friend. After the whole hand shaking, we spent an hour talking about TV shows, Paige, the town...it was nice. But something about him makes me uncomfortable. He's too nice. Too good. And I'm a complete and total fraud.

I walk Paige to school and make sure she's brushing her teeth and doing her homework, but ever since the night with Jared, I've just been going through the motions.

It's almost like depression.

I'm sad because I like our life here, and we're going to have to leave it. I can't help but wonder, what's the point? Why bother with anything?

I don't even drink my coffee on the porch in the morning when Mr. Bingel is out clipping his roses and tending his garden. I avoid everyone, only peeking out the window at eight thirty like a creeper to watch Jared run by.

I'm lucky there haven't been any more thefts or any reason for anyone to really need me. The videos have been useless; even though I've given up checking on them, Paige still looks every day and reviews the tapes.

By the third day of avoidance though, I've apparently gone too far.

"Ruby!" A fist pounds on my door. "Don't make me break your shit. Your lame texts won't keep me away anymore!" It's Tabby.

Every time she's messaged me, I've replied claiming exhaustion. The general avoidance of . . . well, everyone, is over.

I open the door as she's raising her fist again and flinch. "Don't punch me."

She rolls her eyes. "What the hell are you doing? You look like an extra from *The Walking Dead*."

"Thanks."

She frowns and then grabs my hands in her own. Her eyes fix on mine in concern. "Seriously, Ruby. Are you okay?"

"I'm fine."

"Jared's been, like, freaking out. I don't know what his deal is." She shakes her head.

"Really?" The thought sort of perks me up, but it doesn't last long. It's not me he likes, it's Ruby. "I'm okay. Honest. I'm just a little . . ." I shrug. "I don't know, hormonal?"

"Oh, yeah, I get that. I know exactly how to fix it, too." She nods solemnly.

"Margaritas and ice cream?" I think of the last time we hung out.

"No, something even better."

"What's better than booze and sugar?"

"Bingo night."

I laugh and then stop abruptly when I realize she's not laughing with me. "You're not serious."

"As a heart attack. It's at the senior center and most of the people there tonight have had at least one of those so . . . it will be fun, I promise. They're knocking down the old sock emporium at the boardwalk tonight and everything downtown closed early, so it will be super packed and exciting." She gives me a bright grin.

I'm about to protest further, but Paige's voice behind me stops me. "If you go out with Tabby, can I go to Naomi's for the night?" she asks with a pleading smile.

Tabby claps. "That is perfect!" Then she points at me. "You need to shower first though. You smell like you rolled around in rotten potatoes and then slept in garbage."

Before I have a chance to formulate a plausible argument for continuing to live the life of a recluse, she's pushing me up the stairs and into the bathroom.

After I shower, Tabby braids my hair and shoves me into the cleanest clothes she's managed to scrounge up from my room. They must be some of Ruby's leftovers because I'm pretty sure I didn't pack a flowery sundress with spaghetti straps and matching strappy sandals.

"You look awesome," Paige tells me before heading over to her friends.

"Do I really need to get this dressed up for bingo?" I ask Tabby.

"Yep."

"You're wearing jeans," I point out.

She rolls her eyes. "We can stop by my house and I'll change on the way there. Now hurry, or we'll be late."

I'm not sure why she makes that sound like a bad thing, but I follow her without argument and we drive to her house. She changes into a fifties-style polka-dot dress and clips her hair into an updo, and then we're on our way to the senior center.

The parking lot is packed. It takes us almost fifteen minutes to find a parking spot and walk to the large building. Once there, we have to wait in line to purchase the bingo cards.

"How does this work, exactly?" I ask while we're waiting.

"You can buy as many cards as you want. They're five bucks each. All the money goes into the pot. They have five winners and whoever gets a bingo splits the pot of money. Well, most of it. They cover expenses first, then the winners get the rest."

There are at least twenty people in line. I stand on my toes and crane my neck to see through the door where the game will be played. The tables are mostly full, and it's not a small space. The whole damn town is here.

"That must be a lot of money."

"It sure is, and I plan to win it."

We reach the front of the line and she buys seven cards.

"That's thirty-five dollars," I tell her.

"I know."

"On a bingo game."

She shrugs. "I don't mess around."

I order one card—I can't even afford that, really—and then follow Tabby into the giant room where the game is held.

It looks like a school cafeteria. There are linoleum floors, long tables, and hard plastic chairs full of bodies, most of which seem to be over the age of seventy.

"I don't think we'll be able to find a spot to sit together,"

Tabby says, standing on her toes and looking around, fanning her face with her array of bingo cards. "Oh, there's Jared!" She grabs my arm and drags me with her.

"Tabby, I don't think—" I try and stop her, tell her that I don't think Jared wants to see me, but she's not listening.

He's sitting next to Mrs. Olsen and Miss Viola. I've never seen Miss Viola awake. Her eyes look teeny-tiny underneath her thick glasses. There's an empty seat next to Jared at the very end of the table, and Tabby pushes me into it.

"Wait. Where are you going?" I ask, but it's too late. She shoves something in my hands and then she's waving at me over her shoulder as she hustles in the opposite direction.

I'm going to kill her.

Might be a bad idea in a giant room full of people while I'm sitting next to a cop.

Instead, I look at what she handed me. "What is this?" I hold up the container Tabby gave me before she bolted.

"It's a dauber," Jared says.

"A what?"

"You use it to mark the corresponding square when they call your number." He holds up his own container, similar to my own except mine has a blue cap and his is red.

"Oh."

He's wearing jeans and a dark blue, long sleeved Henley. The sleeves are pushed up, exposing his muscular forearms, and the blue of his shirt brings out his eyes.

I focus my gaze on my bingo card. He has three bingo cards in front of him. Miss Viola has one and Mrs. Olsen has two.

"How are you?" Jared asks.

"Fine."

What riveting conversationalists we are.

"I don't think you had a chance to meet Miss Viola," he says, introducing me to his neighbor.

"Hello."

"This is Ruby Simpson," he tells her.

"Nice to meet you." I shake her hand gently. It's frail and thin in my hand, like I'm holding an origami hummingbird.

"What was your name again, dear?" she asks when she sits back in her wheelchair.

"Ruby," Jared says louder, leaning toward her.

"Booby?"

"No. Ruby," he says, even louder. His neck flushes red.

I laugh and it effectively subdues my nerves.

In my peripheral vision, Jared's shoulders shake as he tries to hold it in.

"She can call me Booby if she wants to."

"I'll let her know," he says. He smiles and his eyes crinkle, which makes my smile falter and I look down at my card again.

"What?" Miss Viola asks.

"Nothing, Miss Viola," he yells.

"She's as deaf as a post," Mrs. Olsen says on the other side of Miss Viola. "Yelling won't help you, Deputy."

"Did you call me a ghost?" Miss Viola asks.

Mrs. Olsen shakes her head. "She won't get one of those hearings aids because she thinks it makes her unattractive," Mrs. Olsen tells us, yelling across both Miss Viola and Jared in my direction.

My eyebrows lift. Who exactly is she trying to attract? She's ninety if she's a day. But there's no time for further conversation because a man in a cowboy hat at the front of the room gets on the microphone and tells us it's time to play bingo.

There are a few announcements about other activities at the

senior center, but the crowd gets restless quickly and the cowboy gets the ball rolling on the bingo numbers.

He has an assistant, another elderly lady not quite as old as Miss Viola. She spins the clear plastic tube full of white balls, pulls the number, and hands it to him to read into the microphone.

"B twenty-six!" the cowboy yells into the microphone.

I uncap my dauber and glance over my numbers as they're called out.

With the one card, I don't have much activity, but glancing around, I see that some people are as ambitious as Tabby, with rows of cards in front of them, dabbing and scanning in a hurry as the numbers are read off.

"Do I have bingo?" Miss Viola asks Jared.

"There haven't been enough numbers called yet for a winner," Mrs. Olsen tells her, waving a hand at her with a frown.

More numbers are called and I find that watching the other players is much more entertaining than playing the game.

"We haven't seen you in a few days. Tabby was getting worried."

"That's funny, she said *you* were getting worried."

There's a snuffle and a snort and my attention is drawn to Miss Viola, whose purple-ish wig is now bobbing and sagging.

She's fallen asleep and she's snoring.

For such a little person who probably has little lungs as well, the wheezing sounds filling the air sure are loud.

Jared and I share a smile before turning toward our cards.

"I was worried." He eyes me sideways.

A smile forms on my face, and I can't help but flush with pleasure at his words. But the contentment is short-lived. He shouldn't worry about me. And I shouldn't be happy that he's worried about me.

A few minutes later there's a whoop and a yell. "Bingo!"

It's Tabby, waving a card in the air and standing on her chair.

Groans of discontent echo all around the giant room and the cowboy quickly calms them down.

"Now everyone just wait a minute here while we check the numbers."

Tabby runs up to the front of the room, winning card in hand, and voices erupt all around while the cowboy and his assistant check her card against what was called.

Then there's some discussion at the front that I can't hear, but Tabby doesn't seem to like it. Her arms flail and her voice escalates. I can't make out the exact words, but they sound rather inflammatory.

They argue for a few more minutes, and then two gentleman—both likely in their seventies if the white hair is any indication—appear up front and escort Tabby out through a door near the front.

She struggles against them a little bit and yells something about a conspiracy as she's exiting, and if my lipreading is correct, there were quite a few four-letter words involved in her departure.

The cowboy gets back on the mic and informs everyone the game will be continuing. He doesn't say anything about Tabby or the results of her supposed bingo, but that doesn't stop people from speculating.

"She's always been a cheater," Mrs. Olsen grumbles.

"They turned on the heater?" Miss Viola, who must have been awoken by all of the commotion, fans herself with one of her bingo cards. "That might explain why it's so hot in here."

"Do you think they'll let Tabby back in?" I ask Jared after a few minutes pass and she hasn't reappeared.

"Probably not." He doesn't seem concerned. A number is called and he daubs his own card and then checks Miss Viola's. She's nodding off in the chair next to him again, her purple wig bobbing on her head. "This isn't the first time she's been kicked out."

"She cheated before?"

"I think so. She also got kicked out for accusing other people of cheating and ripping up their cards. She's pretty competitive."

"I guess so. She's also my ride home."

He's silent through two number calls.

"If she doesn't wait for you, I'll drive you home."

"Okay. Thanks."

One corner of his mouth lifts slightly.

The game continues. Miss Viola starts snoring again, softly at first and then progressively louder.

Jared and I exchange fleeting glances full of mirth, and I struggle to hold in my laughter.

But then he's nudging her awake. "Bingo," he says in her ear.

I glance down at her card. She only has two spaces daubed —the ones Jared did since he's been running her card for her— but there's a card with a line right in a row, one of Jared's cards, and he quickly swaps hers for his. "Bingo," he says again in her ear, louder.

"Bingo?" She snuffles out of sleep into wakefulness.

"Bingo," he says again, even louder.

"Bingo!" she yells, fully awake now.

He stands and pushes her to the front. Her purple wig is slightly askew, and she's still a bit groggy from sleep but she has a big grin on her face.

The cowboy checks her numbers and declares her the winner after a few moments of double- and triple-checking. There are groans and shuffles from the remaining participants, but the cowboy assures everyone that they will start the next game after a break, and in the meantime everyone can all enjoy the cakes and treats made by the women's book club.

A group of women are putting out cookies and baked goods on a long table in the back and I ask Jared, "Are you staying?"

He shakes his head. "It's best to leave now while everyone is still here instead of trying to fight through the crowds when they all exit at once." He stands. "Come on, let's see if Tabby is out there waiting for you."

We move through the crowd of people getting in line for cake.

Everyone knows Jared and it takes us a while to exit the building. Every two feet, people stop him to talk and shake his hand.

"Thanks for your help at the hospital the other day, Deputy," a woman says.

Then from the cowboy who was calling numbers up front, "Oh Deputy, we were hoping you'd come to our barbeque this Sunday to thank you for your help at the senior center."

"The ladies at the auxiliary were hoping you'd come model for us again, Deputy." This from two elderly women, one of whom is giggling behind her hand.

He nods. "I can do that."

"Modeling?" I ask.

"They have an art class," he explains.

My brows lift. "Really?"

"It's not a nude," he says, making the ladies titter.

"We would be okay with it if it was," the woman calls out as we're walking away.

He stops and spends time with everyone, waving off their thanks and then introducing me to new people as his friend and the owner of the new shop in town.

By the time we get out of the building, I'm thoroughly convinced the man is a saint.

"Is there anyone you haven't helped here in town?" We've passed through the full parking lot and we're walking along the sidewalk toward where Tabby parked, which is a couple of blocks away. There are street lamps every thirty feet or so, but they're dim.

He shrugs. "It's my job."

"It's your job to volunteer at the hospital and the senior center and the schools in your spare time?"

"Well. No. Where did you say Tabby parked?"

"Stop trying to change the subject. I think we parked on the next block."

"Here's my car." He clicks a button on the keys in his hand and the lights of his Jeep blink. He opens the door for me to get in. "We can drive over there and see if she's left."

I comply, but this conversation isn't over.

He gets in and we drive over to the other block. I point out where Tabby's car was. Now there's an empty space.

"She left me," I say, dismayed.

"She knew I would take you home."

She sure did. That bitch.

"Why did you give your bingo card to Miss Viola?" I ask when we're driving down the dark streets.

In the glow of the lights from the dashboard, he looks uncomfortable. "She needs it more than I do," he finally answers after a moment of silence.

I can't help but gape at him.

He's just so . . . *good*.

I stare at him, flabbergasted, and realize that I am completely turned on.

Which really pisses me off.

Chapter Twenty-Two

W

HEN WE GET to my house, he walks me to the door.

"You don't have to walk me in," I say, still a bit ornery toward him and all his white-knight goodness. My tarnished and checkered history weighs on me, a million times worse in comparison. Plus, I don't need this, this . . . unrequited crap. Why do I want this man so much right now? This cop? This is a horrible decision. He needs to leave before I do or say something stupid.

"I want to make sure you get in okay."

I unlock the door and stomp inside.

"Is everything all right?" He follows me inside, shutting the front door behind him.

"It's fine." In the kitchen, I open the fridge, examining the contents for something that will make me feel better, but there's no alcohol. Just lemonade. It will have to do. I pull the jug out of the fridge and set it on the counter.

"You're not acting like you're fine. Why don't you tell me what's wrong?"

Ignoring him, I open the cupboard where the tall glasses are, but they're on the top shelf. I reach for them, but I know it's futile and the stool is on the other side of the kitchen where Jared's standing, watching me with those dark eyes.

Refusing to give up or turn around, I continue to stretch up on my toes, reaching for the glass.

He comes up behind me, plucks the glass off the shelf and then sets it down on the counter in front of me.

His hands are on either side of my body.

"Ruby," he says, his voice soft.

That makes me even madder.

Quit calling me Ruby. My name isn't Ruby!

I face him, my arm brushing his chest with the turn because he's so close.

He doesn't step back.

"I know why you're upset," he says.

"You do?"

"You can tell me."

Uh, no I can't.

I search his eyes. Whatever it is he thinks he knows, he's wrong. If he knew the truth, he wouldn't be staring down at me with that face, like he can save me like he saves everyone else in this town. He should be arresting me.

I shake my head. "You should go."

"You can trust me."

"I do trust you." The lie slips out without much thought. Do I really trust anyone?

He shakes his head, frustration making his eyes narrow on me. "Then tell me the truth."

My heart thuds in my chest. "What do you mean?"

Does he know? He can't know.

He doesn't say anything, just stares at me enigmatically. I know this ploy. People can't handle silence and if you make them nervous enough, they'll start talking. He can't trick me with that.

"You don't know anything," I say, hoping the words are true. "You should leave." I duck under his arm and stalk down the hallway.

"Ruby," he calls after me.

"You might be the law, but you're not the boss of me."

Jesus, I sound like a toddler.

I make it to the laundry room, trying to find something to do, anything to get out of his space and make him leave.

I'm pulling clothes from the washer and tossing them into the dryer when he finds me.

He leans against the doorframe, watching my angry movements.

I slam the washer shut when I'm done and flick the dryer on. Humming fills the room and he's in my space again.

"What are you running from?"

My stomach drops, wondering again what he knows, or what he thinks he knows, and how is it so close to the truth? Then again, he could be referring to me running from him.

It would be easy to slip past him and out of the close confines of the small, warm room. He's a foot away, but there's a big enough gap that I could fit, and I know he would let me leave.

But instead, I do something I've never done before. I touch him.

I put my hand on his cheek, my palm brushing the rough stubble on his jaw.

He closes his eyes, his breath suddenly deepening. Without

warning, he grabs me in a rough embrace and his mouth descends on mine.

This is no sweet meeting of lips, but a harsh bruising of mouths, like he wants me so badly and it makes him very, very angry.

Well, the feeling is mutual, asshole.

I give it back as good as I'm getting, pulling at his hair, biting at his lips. He's so amazingly frustrating. And good and kind. I want to palm that goodness like a wallet, steal it for myself and hoard it away, as if kissing him will make that innate integrity take root in me.

He lifts me onto the dryer, his fingers digging into my hips as his mouth devours me.

I wrap my ankles together around his waist, pulling him closer. Ruby's thin dress is no barrier between our bodies, and the pressure of his arousal against me makes me even crazier.

His lips move to my neck and I'm panting and grabbing his hair, ready to pull him back to my mouth, but then there's a sound. A loud, beeping sound.

He pulls back, his hand going to his pants to pull out . . . his phone.

He pushes a button, suppressing the noise. After taking a few deep breaths, he puts the offending item to his ear.

"Reeves," he says, his voice deep and a bit hoarse.

His eyes meet mine. His lips are swollen and his hair is a mess from my hands.

I can't look at him. He's too sexy. My forehead drops to his chest and my eyes shut, breathing heavily.

His free hand tightens on my shoulder.

"Hey, Ben."

I open my eyes. On the floor of my laundry room is a pair of dirt-encrusted sneakers. They are too small to be mine, or even Paige's. Under the dried, caked-on mud, they are red. I've seen those shoes before, somewhere else.

I didn't even notice them until now, I was so distracted by Jared. They must belong to one of the boys from the other day.

"You know how she gets when she loses in any kind of game. She'll get over it."

I chuckle. Tabby must have gone to Ben's to drown her sorrows after being kicked out of the bingo game.

"Yeah, I'll come get her. Just let me know when she gets to be unbearable."

I should be worried about Tabby. I should probably go to Ben's myself and get her, but I'm too distracted by the shoes on the floor.

While Jared is still talking to Ben, I slide off the washing machine, nudging him out of the way so I can bend over and examine the shoes. The laces are stuffed inside, a part of one of them ripped off.

And suddenly, everything becomes clear.

The boys. Their dad isn't just a dead beat. They're *stealing* to live. Have things been so dire for them?

I shut my eyes with a sigh.

Jared hangs up with Ben, and I turn toward him, leaving the shoe on the floor.

There's no time for showmanship or a sit-down fake reading. "Greg and Gary," I say. "They're the ones behind all of the thefts. Do you know anything about their dad? Because I've never seen him."

"Wait, what?" He blinks at me, confused about the sudden subject change. "Greg and Gary?"

"Yes. It's them. They're the ones stealing things and mugging people."

"How do you . . ." He shakes his head, his brows furrowed in confusion. "Where did this come from?"

"I just know, okay? Like I knew about the cupcakes, but this time I'm completely right. You have to believe me." I grab his hands in mine and focus on his eyes, willing him to believe what I'm saying. "We have to find them. Do you know anything about their dad?"

What if they've gotten into something truly dangerous? The thefts have gotten more and more risky. They're way too young to be pulling smash and grabs. If they break into the wrong person's house, something could happen to them. Something worse than being separated or put in the foster system.

"I don't know anything about their parents," Jared says finally.

I'm not sure if he believes me, completely, but he squeezes my hands once and then pulls out his phone.

I follow him to the front room while he calls it in. He paces while he's talking. "Two boys. Greg and Gary. Do you know their last name?"

It takes me a minute to realize he's asking me and not the person on the other line.

I think back. Have they ever told me their name? That day on the boardwalk when I bought Gravy . . .

"Sullivan."

He tells the person on the phone, and then there's more back and forth. It sounds like his dispatcher knows about the family.

"Yeah, I've seen that guy, but not for a while. I thought he skipped town. I didn't know he had kids," he says to the person on the phone. There's a moment of silence and then, "When did he get laid off? Have there been any reports from the school?"

After a minute, he hangs up.

"You're right," he says. "Apparently, their dad was working at a factory outside town. He got laid off over a month ago and bailed."

"And left them behind?"

He doesn't say anything, his lips pressed into a thin line. He turns and stalks to the front door with me close behind.

Once we reach the door, Jared turns and faces me. "Stay here."

"Like hell."

"I have to drive out to his last known address. It might not be pretty."

"I don't care."

There's no time to grab my purse or anything else, no time for anything but locking the front door and running behind him out to his car.

He gives a short, frustrated huff when we reach his car and I'm still behind him, but he still opens the passenger side door for me. "You're going to answer some questions about the boys on the way there."

I don't like his demanding tone, but I also want to be there if something's happened, so I don't argue. "Fine."

He shuts my door and jogs around to his side.

"When was the last time you saw them?" he asks as he shoots down the road. Still less than five miles over the limit though.

"They came over last Monday. They had some chores to do

with Mr. Bingel and they stopped by to see Gravy and clean up because they got caught up in some mud. I let them use the washroom." I shake my head.

"The broken bottles make more sense now," Jared says.

"The dad drinks?"

"That's what I was told. I only saw him a few times at Ben's. I didn't realize he was the boys' father." His voice is full of self-recrimination and remorse.

"It's not your fault. You can't have an eye on every person in this town at every moment. You're only one man."

We're silent and tense as he pulls up to a mobile home in a run-down park on the outskirts of town. The windows are dark. There are no cars parked nearby. In the dim light of a flickering street lamp, I can see papers taped on the door, flapping in the breeze.

"Stay here."

I don't argue this time. He jogs up to the door and knocks, obviously not expecting an answer because he's immediately peering into the windows. He pulls the papers from the door. He tries the handle and after a moment of struggle, it opens. He disappears inside.

I want to follow him, but I don't. I sit there in the darkened car and wait for what feels like forever before he appears again.

"There's no one in there," he tells me when he's back inside the car and buckling up. He hands me the papers that he pulled from the door. Eviction notices, letters of water shut off, power shut off . . . I focus on the dates.

"This eviction notice is from a month ago."

Jared swears. "Why didn't they tell anyone?"

"They're kids, they don't know any better." Panic flickers through me and ignites. "We have to find them."

"I'm sure they're okay. They've been on their own this long, they're going to show up again."

I nod, but something is bothering me. My stomach is churning with anxiety, and I feel like I'm missing something really important.

"Where do you think they've been staying?" he asks, continuing to drive down the road, slower than before, unsure where to go or where to even start.

The small muddy shoes from my laundry room keep flashing in my mind. I know I've seen them someplace before, only they weren't muddy. They were a bright red that didn't match the surroundings.

"The building!"

"What building?"

"The old sock emporium, on the boardwalk, the empty one you said was condemned. They've been staying there."

"Are you sure?" he asks, but he's already picking up speed and turning down a road to take us in that direction. He also pulls out his phone.

"Yes. Remember that day? When you yelled at me when I was in there?"

"I didn't yell at you, but yes."

"I heard them. I thought I was imagining things. But I saw his shoe."

"Whose shoe?"

"Gary's shoe, it was sticking out from behind a shelf. I was going to investigate more, but then you told me to leave."

I'm not sure if he hears my entire sentence. He's already barking at someone on the phone. "I need you to send the closest available unit to the boardwalk to the old sock emporium, right away."

The voice chatters on the other end.

"Tonight? Are you sure? Well, tell them to stop." He hangs up and curses, increasing his speed down the dark road.

"Who was that? Tell who to stop?"

"I called dispatch. Maggie said they're demolishing that building tonight."

My stomach drops. That's right, Tabby told me the same thing. "Tonight?"

"They have to do it at night to avoid affecting traffic to the other businesses."

"Maybe they aren't there. Maybe they know and they stayed somewhere else."

"Maybe. The construction company is required to check the building for people first, but they're kids, they're small. They could be hiding anywhere in that old building."

"What time does the demolition begin?"

"It's supposed to start at ten, but Maggie's trying to get ahold of the company to stop them and we have another unit en route. What time is it now?"

"We have ten minutes," I say. "You need to hurry."

He speeds up until we're doing what feels like ninety all the way to the pier. He even drives onto the wooden boards. Then we're running toward the end of the boardwalk. Jared is faster and I yell at him to just go so he can sprint the final distance.

I can't hear the sounds of construction, so I'm hopeful we've made it in time. By the time I get to the building, Jared's already yelling at the crew assembled there, waving his hands and shouting.

It looks like they haven't started their destruction, but there's a machine on the other side of the building from me that's running and too close for comfort.

One of the workers nods and says something to Jared, and they go running into the empty storefront.

By the time I reach the door to go in after them, Jared's already coming out, and he's alone.

"They aren't there?" I ask.

"They are," he says, his brow furrowed. "They won't come out."

"What?"

"They're underneath, in the basement. The door to the crawlspace is locked. I called out and they answered, but they won't open it."

"Why not?"

"They have a list of demands."

"Are you serious?"

"It makes sense, actually. It explains why they didn't say anything when their dad disappeared. Greg said he knows what happens when CPS gets involved, and he's not leaving his brother."

A few guys from the demolition crew walk by, laughing about something, the sound jarring considering the circumstances.

"Oh my god. Can they stay with me? I can take both of them."

I really can't take both of them, not long-term. Not if I plan on leaving, and I know I'll have to leave eventually. But maybe I can have them until I find a better solution.

"You have to be screened and on the county list to take in kids. And Greg's worried he's going to get in trouble for the thefts."

"They won't, right?" I put my hand on his arm. "They're

just kids. They were trying to support themselves. You can't let them get lost in the system."

"I'll do everything I can for them."

I nod, but my expression must betray my anxiety because he pulls me to him, wrapping his arms around me and talking over my head.

"They'll be tried as juveniles, and the punishment won't be severe. Most likely probation, but I can't guarantee that they'll be placed somewhere together. Their dad is gone, but we'll try to find him. I have to call the county to get them placed tonight with someone who's already been approved. The boys are right. Depending on spots available, they could be separated."

"What's going to happen now?"

"A guy on the crew is checking to see if we can break down the door to get them out without knocking everything down. They already started on the opposite side, and structurally, it might not be safe."

Jared's phone rings and he walks a few steps away to take the call.

The ground shudders underneath me for a brief moment.

What the . . . ? Is that an earthquake? No, it's the building.

There are shouts all around me.

"It's gonna collapse soon!" someone yells.

What about the boys?

I don't wait for Jared to make a decision or get off his phone call. I bolt into the building.

He yells something behind me, but I don't turn around.

It's not hard to find the crawlspace. There are footprints in the dust where the boys have been coming and going.

I knock on the wood.

"Go away unless you're prepared to meet all my demands." Greg. The words are tough, but he sounds scared.

"Greg, it's me."

"Ruby?"

"Yes."

"Are you going to help us?" My heart clenches at Gary's smaller voice.

"I'm going to do whatever I can, I promise. But you guys have to come out of there. This building is going to collapse."

"We can't do that," Greg says. "I'm not letting anyone take my brother from me."

"It's not safe." I try again. "This building is already falling down. Someone could get hurt and then you really won't be together. Didn't you feel the shaking?"

There's silence at that, and then they're whispering to each other. A machine rattles outside, and my heart lurches, my mind racing for a solution.

The ground shakes again, and a corner of the building behind me starts to topple.

I shriek as drywall and dust fall from the ceiling.

"It's going to come down!" I yell into the door.

The latch jiggles.

I'm panicking as the door lifts up. I grab the lid and scramble down in the hole with them, slamming the door shut behind me. I throw my arms over both of them right as the world falls down around us.

Chapter Twenty-Three

IT'S DARK. I can't see anything. My ears ring from the sound of plaster and wood collapsing damn near on top of me.

"Greg? Gary?" I cough out the names.

When I come back to myself, I feel them. My arms are still around them. We're sitting on a hard floor in a narrow space. Their little bodies shake against me.

Greg starts to cough. It feels like we're covered in a cloud of dust.

Holy crap. We're alive.

"Are you guys okay?" I ask when they don't say anything.

One of them nods, the movement of their head brushes my arm. It must be Gary, he feels smaller.

"I'm okay," Greg says on my other side.

I remove my arms from around them, but they stay huddled into my side. I try to assess the damage, but it's too dark to see much of anything.

The basement didn't completely collapse, at least not by the crawlspace door where we are. The area directly above us seems to have held up. I reach out with my hands. We're surrounded by rubble. The only space we have is directly under the trap door, just enough room to sit, with maybe a foot of space above my head and perhaps two feet around us. It's not much.

"Don't worry," I say, "They know we're in here and they'll get us out soon."

I hope.

There's silence for a moment. My ears start to get better, and I listen for the sounds of movement outside the rubble, but I don't hear anything. I shift on the hard step, trying to see how far I can spread my legs out. It's not much. The boys shift with me and we get as comfortable as we can while we wait.

"Should we try to dig out?" Greg asks. He shuffles a bit more next to me.

"No," I say quickly. "We don't want to make more things fall on us. I'm sure they're working hard on getting us out right now. We should stay in one spot to make it easier."

"When we get out of here, will they let us stay together?" Gary asks.

My heart hurts for him.

"I hope so." I have an idea that might work, but I don't want to get their hopes up. "We won't know until we get out of here."

We're silent for a while. Crouched on the ground. Waiting. I try not to think too hard about the small space we're occupying and the layers and layers of wood and dirt and who knows what between us and freedom. Hopefully there's enough air getting in to let us breathe for a while. I shudder.

"They're going to send us to jail," Greg says after a while.

"No!" I want to keep them calm, but I can't lie. "Well . . . You are in a bit of trouble for stealing things, but Jared said since you're so young it will probably just be probation and that sort of thing."

"What's probation?" His poor little voice sounds exhausted.

"It's nothing horrible. It means you'll have to stay in your home for a while and you can only leave to go to school."

"That doesn't sound bad," Gary says. "I want to stay somewhere that's home."

You and me both, kid.

"You aren't mad about us stealing?" Gary asks.

"I'm not mad. How did you guys steal the purse from the lady at the boardwalk without anyone seeing you?"

Greg answers. "I saw it on TV. We took some bags from this old lady who was sleeping. We were using them for blankets, too, because there were so many. The blond lady on the boardwalk, she was distracted and I came up behind her and put it over her head. Gary grabbed her purse and ran back here. Gary is so small, people usually ignore him or don't notice him, anyway. She started screaming though. We didn't mean to frighten her. We never tried doing it again after that."

"How did you get into the gas station?"

Greg answers again. "We snuck into the back room and hid behind some boxes until they closed."

That's why there was no sign of a break-in.

I ask the question, even though I can surmise the answer. "Why did you break all the bottles?"

Greg answers. "Our dad cared more about those bottles than he did us."

We're all quiet for a few minutes after that statement. Then, "Why didn't you guys ask someone for help?"

"We don't want to be separated," Gary says.

"We've heard stories about kids in foster homes," Greg continues. "People are mean to them. We don't want to have to leave Castle Cove. What if our dad comes back for us?"

I swallow. Their dad returning doesn't seem like the best-case scenario in my head, but they are just kids.

Gary falls asleep next to me, leaning onto my arms, his breathing fanning my wrist.

I think I start to doze, too, when there's a loud bang and light starts streaming in through cracks in the door above us.

"I think they're getting closer," I tell the boys.

The noise wakes up Gary and he starts crying, quiet little hiccups and sniffles.

I hold him tighter. "It's okay. It will be over soon." They both huddle closer to me.

There's more noise from above and then the door is wrenched open.

I blink against the light shining in. It's not the sun; we haven't been in there that long. It's some kind of giant spotlight.

"Thank god," a voice says.

Arms reach in for the boys. I do my best to help them out first, and then it's my turn. I can barely stand; my legs are asleep and numb from sitting on the hard floor for who knows how long.

Strong arms pull me out.

It's Jared and he's hugging me.

"Are you okay?"

"Yes, we're fine."

"I tried to go in the building after you, but they wouldn't let me. Don't *ever* do that again." He sounds pissed. But a weird pissed, like angry and relieved all at once.

Time passes in a blur of activity. Someone throws a blanket around me and I'm walked and mostly carried over to a waiting ambulance with the boys. An EMT checks me out and declares me fit to leave, but it seems to take forever. Jared is nearby at all times, either with me or the boys as we're being poked and prodded.

When I finally have a minute, I turn to Jared. "The boys," I tell him. "They want to stay together."

"I know," he says. "I called the county and they're sending a worker out. They'll need emergency placement—"

"Mr. Bingel."

"What?"

"Trust me. Call Mr. Bingel."

He frowns at me, a confused line appearing between his eyes, but he agrees. "Okay."

~

"How did you know about Mr. Bingel?" Jared asks me.

We're standing on my porch. Well, he's standing on my porch. I've unlocked the door and I'm halfway inside, wondering if Jared wants to come in with me.

It's a terrible, horrible, wonderful idea for so many reasons.

Hours have passed since we emerged from the basement of the abandoned building. The boys are safely next door. The sun is rising. I waited until the boys' situation was resolved until I let Jared take me home.

I shrug at his question. "When in doubt, know the future." I put my purse on the ground just inside the door and turn to face him, leaning against the doorframe.

"That's very funny. Seriously though. I had no idea he had registered as a foster parent."

I smile and say nothing.

He's quiet for a moment, standing there, not leaving, but not coming in either, shifting on his feet like he always does when he's uncomfortable. He clears his throat. "About earlier . . ."

"What about it?"

"I shouldn't have . . . I didn't mean to take advantage of the situation."

I can't help but smile. "You think you took advantage of me?"

"No, I just mean, since we're working together and everything, we probably shouldn't do . . . that."

"We shouldn't make out in my laundry room," I clarify.

"Yes, right. I mean, no. I mean, it's not the best idea—"

"Jared."

"What?"

"Do you want to come in?"

He stares at me, his gaze as intense as ever. I flush under the weight of his scrutiny.

Then he steps over the threshold.

To be continued . . .

Ready for book two? Available now! Check out Too Much Crime on My Hands at a retailer near you!

About the Author

Go here to sign up for the newsletter!
www.authormaryframe.com

Mary Frame is a full-time mother and wife with a full-time job. She has no idea how she manages to write novels except that it helps being a dedicated introvert. She doesn't enjoy writing about herself in third person, but she does enjoy reading, writing, dancing, and damaging the eardrums of her coworkers when she randomly decides to sing to them. She lives in Reno, Nevada, with her husband, two children, and a border collie named Stella.

She LOVES hearing from readers and will not only respond but likely begin stalking them while tossing out hearts and flowers and rainbows! If that doesn't creep you out, email her at:
maryframeauthor@gmail.com
Follow her on Twitter: @marewulf
Like her Facebook author page: www.
facebook.com/AuthorMaryFrame

Imperfect Series reading order:
Book One: Imperfect Chemistry
Book Two: Imperfectly Criminal
Book Three: Practically Imperfect

Book Four: Picture Imperfect
Book Five: Imperfect Strangers
Book Six: Imperfectly Delicious

Looking for more nerdy romance?
Check out this dorky spin-off duet!
The Dorky Duet (Plus a companion novel!)
Rirdorkulous
Geektastic
Nerdelicious

Castle Cove Mystery Series
Fake it to the Limit
Too Much Crime on My Hands
You're the Con That I Want

Time After Time series
Time of My Life
If I Could Turn Back Time

Fox Family Series
Between a Fox and a Hard Place
The Fox and the Rebound

www.ingramcontent.com/pod-product-compliance
Lightning Source LLC
Chambersburg PA
CBHW030623190726
48286CB00008B/2377